EX-ARMY MAN
TURNS RENEGADE!

But here in a hot and panicky fight, with war arrows whirring through the air, and crazily yelling Sioux trying to kill a bucking mule, Sam wasn't able to think or move calmly. He knew that he was caught without a weapon for the defense of the woman and himself unless he could recover the knife which he'd dropped. He wished that he hadn't laid the old Henry down on that hot rock. . .

Only place for women is in town. You can buy 'em a drink or so, dance and have a good time with 'em. But leave 'em behind when you hit the trail. . .

We will send you a free catalog on request. Any titles not in your local book store can be purchased by mail. Send the price of the book plus 50¢ shipping charge to Leisure Books, P.O. Box 270, Norwalk, Connecticut 06852.

Titles currently in print are available for industrial and sales promotion at reduced rates. Address inquiries to Nordon Publications, Inc., Two Park Avenue, New York, New York 10016, Attention: Premium Sales Department.

BULLET SONG

W.F. Bragg

LEISURE BOOKS ❧ NEW YORK CITY

A LEISURE BOOK

Published by

Nordon Publications, Inc.
Two Park Avenue
New York, N.Y. 10016

To All The Lauras

CHAPTER I

Three hairy men in dingy buckskin slipped silently through the lodge-pole pine timber. The last man in line led the shaggy saddle horses. On their back trail, well concealed in thicker timber, they had tied up the string of pack ponies laden with their spring catch of beaver pelts. Although they moved as noiselessly as their shadows, Singin' Sam Sling advanced too boldly for the comfort of his comrades.

The scrawny old man with the ragged beard piloting the horses admonished Sam when they checked in a green mountain park for a breather. "You'll lose your hair sure, Sam, if yuh don't slow down. I can smell Sioux bucks plain as all git-out."

Sam twitched his long sunburnt nose, savouring the air. About him was a youthful look, despite the deep lines in his gaunt brown face, and the coarse black hair that fell to his greasy collar.

"I smell smoke," he replied. "What wind there is comes from the direction of our winter camp. Shorty, maybe Buffalo Hump and his squaw need help right bad."

"If a Sioux war party jumped our camp," Shorty argued, "time's long past to help Hump and the Night Star. Better for us to go slow and see what started the smoke down thar."

The third man of the party, a short-coupled Indian, was squatting on lean hams, peering through a break in the timber that offered a view of the quiet beaver meadow just below the lodge-poles.

"What you think, Tom?" Sam asked. "We spotted that smoke from up on the divide this mornin'. You figure we're goin' too slow? Night Star's your sister. A pretty squaw worth savin' from these Sioux war whoops."

Tom Bear Mouth shook his head.

"Smoke look bad," he answered, in his broken Agency English. "But can't see yet where come from."

"Let's git to where we can see then," Sam said impatiently.

"Go fast, Sioux see us first, they there," argued Tom.

"But think of your sister, Tom. Maybe she's holed up in the shack or around the cache, along with Hump, just prayin' for us to come fast."

"We see smoke long time now. Too late for pray if Sioux down there."

Rocky Mountain Shorty Gadberry, chewing tobacco, minding the ponies so that they would not snort or whinny, broke into the powwow. "You're too hot-livered, Sam. You go bustin' along like a blind hawg in a root cellar, and shore as all git-out, them Sioux'll make bridle tassels out'n your hair. Anyway, it's not a cinch bet that smoke's comin' from our winter camp. Might be somethin' else in the woods. We work along easy through this timber, and right quick we'll git to whar' we can look things over a hull lot. If Sioux bucks is tryin' to hide out, we'll see 'em soon as they spot us. Maybe sooner. And if so," he slapped the barrel of his heavy Sharps buffalo gun, "Susy, here, 'll git in the first lick."

"Ain't been a thunder and lightnin' storm all this June to start a fire," said Sam. "Smoke don't come from no cook fire built by Night Star. She's too smart to use wood that makes smoke. She'd do her cookin' with quakin' asp. So— leavin' out lightnin'—somebody built the fire that raised that smoke down there. And it's my belief that somebody was a bunch of Sioux raidin' our winter camp."

Sam Sling knew well enough his two friends were offering sane counsel, but a heavy feeling of guilt had oppressed him since dawn when the smoke had first been seen. The trappers had gone to the high country, leaving Buffalo Hump and his wife in charge of the camp, presumably well hidden in a patch of quakers, and the cache filled with the fall take of beaver pelts, and carefully concealed. The trapping party had planned for a stay of three weeks away from camp but had cut short the work, gathered traps and furs, packed horses, and headed downcountry at sight of the thin streamer of smoke.

Sam's feeling of guilt came from the fact that he had led the party into this timbered country in the southern part of the Big Horn Mountains the fall before. Mountain streams, of late years, had been trapped out, but he had heard of this secluded stream on which white men had not set out a single trap. Trouble was that this country lay within territory set aside for the Sioux tribes by federal treaty. Even though General Custer, this year, had reported discoveries of gold in the Black Hills, army troops continued to bar white settlers from the vast land north of the North Platte, bounded by the Big Horns on the west, and the Black Hills to the east. The Bozeman Trail to the Montana gold fields had been blocked. The Indians had even burned down the hated forts, C. F. Smith and Phil Kearny.

But Tom Bear Mouth, Buffalo Hump, and the Night Star were from the Shoshone tribe now camped far west in the Wind River country. Enmity over hunting territory ran between the Sioux and the Shoshones. The latter tribe also laid claim to this area where Sam had found a beaver bonanza. It had not been difficult to persuade the Indians to come along on the expedition. Rocky Mountain Shorty had been more cautious, but he had at last given in to Sam's coaxing, since the two whites had been partners for the past four years from the Canadian line to the Mexican border, trapping and hunting.

"I can't take it so slow," Sam said. "I just got to find out what's happened." He walked over to his blaze-faced, buckskin pony, Baldy. He took the bridle reins from Shorty's hand, and reached for a stirrup. His Henry forty-four calibre magazine rifle was in its saddle boot, his Colt six-gun chambered to take similar-sized shells, hung from Sam's belt.

Tom Bear Mouth shook his head and muttered, "White brave." Which Sam understood as indicating that, in the Indian's opinion, he was foolhardy.

B.S.—1*

Shorty worked his whiskered jaws on his tobacco, watching his partner mount Baldy. He made no offer to board his own pony and follow Sam's lead.

"By cracklin'," he declared, "I don't know what yuh aim to do, gallivantin' around on a hoss in this timber, but me and Tom'll foller along slow. If we hear shootin', we'll try to figure out somethin'. But don't count too much on us. Might be a hull pack of Sioux down thar."

Shorty and Tom were brave enough, Sam knew, but being uncertain as to the size of the Sioux war party, they would not run undue risk before they gained plenty of information. They were frontier veterans. They had fought the Sioux before this, and they had no illusions—as did some of the greenhorn soldiers manning the Powder River country outposts—that one white man could whip ten Indians.

"Somehow or other, if I think they're hid out down there," said Sam, "I'll try and get a count on 'em."

"Maybe they already took tally on us and have built that smoke to drag us into a trap," Shorty said shrewdly. "If they have got the Hump and Night Star, maybe they know we're still somewhere in these hills, and they're tryin' to wipe us all out."

"It's a mile down to camp." Sam kicked Baldy in the ribs with moccasined heels. "I can nigh walk fast as this cayuse where timber's thick. Keep your eyes and ears open. If you decide things have gone plumb wrong for me and the others, pull your freight out'n the mountains."

They parted without shaking hands. Frontier partners were not long on sentiment. All Shorty said, as Sam rode away, was, "Keep your hair on straight, bub."

Sam trusted his pony, for Baldy was a prized hunting horse, broken to stand under gunfire when buffalo kills were made by the partners, or skirmishes waged with roving Indians. Baldy would even pack a freshly killed grizzly bear pelt back of the saddle, which, Sam knew, was about top performance for a pony.

Sam's problem was to reach a position where he could scout

out the location of the winter camp in its quaking asp patch. The timber thinned out along this lower flank. As he rode along, with Baldy picking his way carefully through raspberry brush, and around obstructing mossy green down logs, like a well trained bird dog. Sam could catch occasional glimpses of the beaver meadow to his left. It was a quiet green bowl, early June grass fragrant and moist along a clear trout stream, velvety sheen starred with the yellow of buttercups, and the blue of mountain daisies.

Gentle slopes fingered down from the timber to the meadow. But Sam knew that he must break into the open and work his way far down one of these pitches before he could set eye on the camp hideout. Willow brush grew thickly along the stream, offering good concealment if Sioux warriors had raided the camp, then hidden out to ambush the three trappers.

Sam knew that so far as they were able, Shorty and Tom would be following slowly along his trail, straining their eyes at every step to discover his whereabouts or sign of the Indians.

If it hadn't been that he blamed himself for bringing the Hump and his pretty Indian wife into these lonely mountains, Sam would not have started this bold ride against unknown odds. He knew, also, that if disaster had overtaken the expedition, no aid or redress could be secured from the nearest army post which was Cantonment Sparks, far to the east on a fork of the North Platte River.

Sam and Shorty were outside the law, taking beaver on Sioux treaty land. The three Shoshones might believe they possessed a justifiable trapping right up here, but Shoshone claims to this particular section had not been allowed in the treaty. If the Sioux had killed Buffalo Hump and Night Star, they would not be outside the law so far as the army was concerned.

As Baldy nosed along, Sam kept a weather eye peeled, watching his left flank where occasional openings in the timber gave him a good view of the beaver meadow. The sun was almost noon high, and the valley slept peacefully under the balmy June sky. Once he saw a doe across the stream feeding along the edges of blue timber. She sighted the lanky frontiersman on the buckskin pony, and pricked up her mule-like ears.

He wasn't more than fifty yards now above the quaker patch where the winter shack had been built. The wind was light and warm, but it was blowing straight toward Sam. It was rank with the smell of smoke.

Dismounting, he dropped the ends of his reins to the earth. his pony was trained to stand without being tied by the head. He drew the Henry from its rawhide sheath and carefully checked for action and full magazine. Old Shorty swore by Susy, his single-shot fifty calibre buffalo gun, averring it wasn't filled up with new-fangled machinery like a repeater that would jam up and let a man down in a pinch. Shorty could knock over a buffalo at six hundred yards with his Sharps. But Sam had a high respect for the Henry and the Colt hand gun.

He edged from the timber, hiding in brush and shadows cast by the tall pines wherever cover offered. But he felt quite certain that if Sioux were cached out in the beaver meadow, they had long since spotted him moving down-country. He was running chances to get to a place where he could see the camp location. A scantily timbered point stretching down toward the creek obscured his vision. He must get low enough to see around the trees.

The smell of the smoke had informed his nose that more than wood had been set afire. Under Shorty's teaching, Sam had schooled eyes and ears and nose on the frontier. Wood smoke, for instance, smelt different from that from burning cloth or blankets. Sam could smell a distinct odour of burnt cloth on the wind.

He came out to where cover was no longer possible. He estimated that he was about a hundred horse jumps—long ones—from a bushy bend of the creek. The willows grew thickly enough there to hide twenty or thirty men and horses.

The brush was ribboned with narrow trails trodden by browsing deer and elk. Skilled riders could move around in it under hiding.

This bright land, as a general rule, rang in spring time to the songs of little mountain birds that loved the grass and the streams. Song birds were not sounding off today. Instead, as Sam finally reached a point where he could take a gander at the spot in the slope where they had dug the beaver cache, a flock of large black and white birds flapped off across the meadow, squawking harshly.

They were magpies. They were meat birds. Something around the cache or the camp in the quakers had aroused the curiosity or—more likely—their appetite. Then Sam had appeared, frightening them. They were alarming the wilderness.

CHAPTER II

Sam's heart missed a beat as, from the corner of his eye, he saw a black hole in the grassy slope where the beaver cache had been dug. That wasn't all he saw in that brief glance. Something warm and brown, something that resembled a naked human leg, protruded from the cache. The flesh gleamed under the June sun.

The time was past now for Sam Sling to hide out and ponder and wonder if the Sioux were down in the willows. Tom Bear Mouth had termed him white brave and he knew that his impulsive nature had gained him a reputation, even among enemy Indians, of foolhardiness. He was also a man of imagination, a sort of rude frontier bard. It had long been his custom to while away dreary hours in winter camps, singing frontier ballads or, when his repertoire ran thin, composing his own verses to familiar music. The Shoshones knew all about his singing, for all Indians like to sing. And quite likely the Sioux also had heard about Singin' Sam

Sling, for Indian gossip ran over the plains and mountains like pale-face chatter in a New England village.

Sam wanted to draw the Indians from the brush. These Sioux were proud men. He whipped up the Henry and cracked a couple of slugs into the brush. He began to sing his own song as he advanced slowly down the slope on his knee-high moccasins stained with beaver blood and horse sweat.

> "Oh—take me back to the buff'ler days,
> When Injuns whooped in the prairie haze,
> Deadwood gold shined in the pan,
> The range was free to every man."

That last line referred to Sam's contempt for army regulations on treaty land trespassing. When his hoarse song had wound up, he began to taunt the Sioux, telling them they were women who preferred to hide in the brush rather than come out and fight a long hair. He advised them to go back to camp and help the squaws gather wood and water. They could send out the little boys of the tribe to do their fighting. He punctuated his jeering talk with snapping bullets. He broke down Sioux patience. They broke from cover, a dozen naked painted men on hard-running ponies. They rushed Sam. He stood his ground, Henry held ready for a target. The leading buck, who rode a yellow pony, pulled a bow string to his ear and drove an arrow through the slack of Sam's shirt. He felt the fiery burn of the arrow head on his short ribs.

In a tight like this one, a man couldn't waste time pulling out an arrow head. The ground shook to the soft thunder of the scampering unshod hoofs on the thick sod. Singin' Sam, dropping to one knee, counted a dozen wild riders in the line of horsemen. He could see the red, green, and black war paint on the faces and bodies of the warriors. They charged straight up the gently rising slope, bending and swaying, to throw the long hair who faced them off his line of aim.

The brave, who had shot Sam with the arrow, galloped a half-dozen paces in the lead. He was naked except for paint and breech clout. He had fastened a bunch of feathers and a war medicine bag of otter skin to the streaming black tail of his yellow pony. Squinting his eyes against the sun glare, Sam decided this buck was a war chief and the most likely target for the Henry.

The arrow wound was burning like the pangs of hell. The shaft, sticking out of his flapping buckskin shirt, hampered Sam's fighting action some, but not too much. He hoped that Shorty and Tom Bear Mouth were somewhere up in the timber, near enough by this time to get a count on the strength of the war party.

Sam figured he had done his good deed for the day. He had taunted the Sioux into exposing their strength. They had carefully set their trap, but Sam had sprung it prematurely with his buffalo song and taunts about Sioux courage.

He felt a bit nervy as he waited for the ponies to come near enough so that he could see the white rims of their walled eyes. Many a greenhorn had lost his hair while adventuring across the Great Plains by emptying his rifle before the foe had come within good shooting distance.

The Sioux were barking out their wolfish war whoops as they rode. The shrill echoes, and the crack of the few guns that were carried by the warriors, rang back from the rocky rims of the valley. Even if Shorty and Tom couldn't see, they would hear the fight. Whether they would pull out of the hills immediately or come to Sam's aid was a question that Sam had no time now to worry about.

He ran a good chance of losing his hair right here in this pretty little mountain meadow where he had spent a passable winter in fairly comfortable quarters, fleshing and stretching a good stake in fur.

It was amazing, he reflected fleetingly, how much a man could think about in the short space of time that had been given him since he jumped the Sioux and they snapped an arrow into the meat over his short ribs. If he got wiped out here, he wondered how soon word would get to his brother, Rick, somewhere down around Fort Fred Steele with Sam's former infantry company. Rick would feel sorry, no doubt, but he would not be surprised, for he had given his wild young brother up for lost when the latter threw in with Rocky Mountain Shorty.

And then Sam wondered, too, how the Sioux had come to know just where the beaver pelts were hidden away. That cache had been cunningly dug and concealed. So far as Sam knew, nobody had even known the fall before that the party was adventuring into this part of the Big Horns. But somewhere, somehow, the Sioux had found out. And they had bided their time, then struck like wild hawks falling from the sky on crouching rabbits.

The buck on the yellow pony was near enough now, Sam decided. He could feel the smooth brown stock of the Henry against his cheek. The hammer was drawn to full cock and the pressure of finger on trigger felt comforting to Sam. He looked through the sights at this short range. The Sioux chief was a bold one: a broad-built, lanky rider, with a single eagle feather in his black hair. On his naked breast was painted a medicine sign in blood red that looked to Sam like a crude figure of a pitching pony.

Sam socked his knee into the sod for a steadier stance. This move proved unwise. He had momentarily, in the heat of the fight, forgotten the arrow sticking in his flesh. He flinched as he fired—and knew, as he pulled off, that he had not blown that painted medicine sign off the oncoming buck's breast as had been his intent.

He dumped the rider off the yellow pony, but he knew he had not made a clean kill. For the buck bunched up and rolled like a spitting wildcat into the cover of a clump of raspberry brush the moment he struck the ground. The yellow pony pop-eyed with fear, rushed on past Sam toward the timber, dragging from its lower jaw a long rawhide thong of the war bridle.

Sam wanted to sing but he couldn't spare breath for it. He jumped up on his long legs. He was firing rapidly, barely flipping rifle stock to shoulder before he snapped the hammer.

Indians hated point-blank fire. They had shown the long hair they were not afraid to come out and fight. Maybe they'd go back in the brush now and try for a starve-out on Sam.

He was counting on that. He sprayed the oncoming line of braves with his lead. He knocked over a pony at the far end of the line, and saw another whooping rider go spinning headlong into the sod. They had come in so near now that he could see the big round eyes of the ponies, and their flaring red nostrils. Smoke from the Henry circled up, but the haze could not hide the painted faces of the Sioux, their mouths wide open as they shrilled their defiance.

When he killed the pony, he broke the heart of this first rush. They veered off to both flanks, swinging low so that the bodies of their ponies barricaded them from this long hair's far reaching bullets. They dashed down to the stream and into the willow brush.

Never taking time for a breather, Sam turned and made a headlong run toward the looted beaver cache. The hole was a good six feet deep, he knew well. He had helped to dig it. When his moccasins touched the rim, he took a header into the cavity.

He crouched for a moment, panting like a hard-run hound, feeling the hammering of his heart against his ribs, feeling, too, the white-hot burn of that confounded arrow head. Knowing they'd try another rush if he didn't show himself in fighting position, he staggered up, and laid the hot barrel of the Henry on the edge of the pit.

He saw the pony he had killed, still kicking in its death agony not far down the grassy slope and to his right. Apparently the Sioux were in the willows, also getting their breath, planning the next move against the long hair who sang so boldly.

Sam's first move was to reload his rifle, then check on the spare ammunition in his shell belt and the "possibles" leather pouch he carried on his belt.

His hasty check showed that he possessed thirty rounds of soft-nosed forty-fours which would kill a heap of Sioux. He lined the shells up on the edge of the pit within easy reaching distance if he were forced to reload hurriedly. Man never knew about Indians. They might try another headlong charge if he could work them up to it. His jeers had flushed them before. This sun was getting pretty hot and Sam's mouth began to feel as if it were filled with cotton. He heard the soft chuckle of creek water down there, rippling over stones, and licked his parched lips.

And he became aware, too, as the fighting fog cleared from his brain and the pain of his wound increased, that he was not the only person inside the looted beaver cache. The owner of the brown leg also occupied part of the pit. Sam felt the gentle pressure against the back of his legs. He could feel the skin crawling on the back of his neck as he made a wary circle.

The naked body had been crammed, head down, into the pit. The face and head were hidden from Sam because a metal water bucket had been pushed down over the head. But Sam saw, from the bodily contours, that this was not the Indian woman, not Tom Bear Mouth's sister, the Night Star. Quite likely this was her husband, the Buffalo Hump.

A touch of the flesh gave Sam's hand a clammy feeling. The Hump had been dead for several hours. Not far distant to the rear of the cache loomed the quaking asp patch in which had been built the log winter shack. Rank smoke still eddied from the grove. Sam's heart felt as cold now as the Hump's dead body. He was wondering about the fate of the Night Star.

The shaft of the arrow, sticking out of Sam's hunting shirt, bothered him. He seized it and gave a mighty pull, hoping he could dislodge the head. But he felt his toes curl up and the icy sweat run down the insides of his legs. The arrow head wouldn't come out of his meat. It was there for keeps, at least until Sam could find time to remove his shirt and operate with his skinning knife.

When the sharp pain of his lacerated flesh had died down he took a deep breath, gripping the shaft firmly with his left hand. Then, using his knife, he hacked off the shaft up near his body. Now he could swing around in his pit without a jarring of the wound each time the shaft touched the dirt walls.

He hated to take another look at the Buffalo Hump, for the brown body, smeared with half-dried blood, kept reminding him. He had laughed and called them a pack of squaws. He would remove the Hump from the pit, but the Sioux were giving him no time for that.

Sam had sung for the Sioux. Now they sang for him. He understood enough of the lingo to know they were taunting him. He had laughed and called them a pack of squaws. He had dared them to come out and fight like men. Well, they had come out. But the long hair, the bold singer, he had not stayed very long to fight. He had run and jumped into a hole like a prairie-dog. The Sioux sang to Sam Sling that this amazed them, for they had believed he could stand up and catch bullets in his hands, and that his medicine was very strong. But it looked as though the Sioux had been mistaken. He was a prairie-dog, not a bold big medicine singer. He had gone into his hole. He wouldn't come out.

The combined pangs of the arrow head wound and thirst put a wire edge on Sam's temper.

He vowed that he wouldn't shoot recklessly nor expose himself unless he saw a fair chance to down a couple of Sioux. When the warriors understood they could not draw him from his hole with mockery, they fell silent. Sam knew they were planning new tactics. They might attempt another rush but he didn't think so. They had left a dead pony sprawled in the grass. And he had sent their chief crawling into that patch of berry brush and rocks over to his left front. Sam wondered if the chief was still hiding there. He couldn't see a ripple of movement in the bushes to indicate that the man lived.

CHAPTER III

But with the cold feeling of Hump's body against the back of his legs, poetic fancy didn't come easily to Sam's mind. Besides, the Sioux tried another trick on him. Far down the valley, a good two hundred yards away, three of the painted horsemen cantered out of the brush. The one who led waved a long feathered lance over his head. Something black, like a bundle of tarred rope, dangled from the tip of the lance.

The Sioux, who were hiding in the brush, taunted Sam anew, explaining to him that the black object on the lance was the scalp of the Buffalo Hump. The Hump, they pointed out, had been dishonoured by being scalped. When the warrior who had killed him died and went to the Happy Hunting Grounds, the Hump would be his slave for eternity.

But if Sam Sling could take the hair of the killer of the Hump, then the Hump would live on honourably in the Indian paradise. They were telling the truth to Sam. He knew enough about their beliefs to understand that. They were inviting him to kill the warrior who toted the lance, and avenge his scalped friend.

They succeeded in arousing Sam's anger anew. He studied the three horsemen closely. They were within range of the Henry but they were not aware of the carrying power of Sam's gun. These Sioux were armed for the most part with old trade muskets, guns with worn-out barrels from which they fired lead slugs they had moulded. Some of the Sioux lately were picking up magazine rifles and fixed ammunition, but finding it difficult since few white men would furnish them with modern firearms.

The Indian rider, who trailed the carrier of the scalp, trotted nearer to Sam. He came out into a patch of sunlight which revealed that he was wearing a blue army blouse.

Brass buttons flashed in the sun. Sam was keen-eyed, and could even make out white chevrons on the sleeves indicating that the former owner of the blouse had been an infantry non-commissioned officer.

The leading Sioux singer in the willow patch now informed Sam that the coat had come from a walkaheap soldier down on the Platte River who had foolishly attempted to ride a pony. Walkaheaps were not men enough to ride horses, so the Sioux had stampeded the pony and the soldier had been thrown off and lost his coat.

This song wound up with a brassy sound that amazed Sam. It was the bray of an army bugle. That had been Sam's first job when he was a young army kid. He had been a wind-jammer with the infantry. And he had never known an Indian who could pucker up his lips expertly enough to blow a bugle. Either a white man had shown a Sioux buck how to sound a bugle, or a white renegade was with this war party. The fleeting thought came to Sam that this might also explain why the Sioux had been able to find the winter camp. It was just possible that Sam or his partner had dropped an unwise hint which had set some renegade on their trail into the Big Horns.

He had been willing enough to take his discharge and get away from army red tape and regulations. But many men still served in the army who were his friends. Nor could Sam forget that his older brother also wore infantry chevrons. For the honour of his old regiment, he would risk one bullet on the wearer of the blue coat.

He switched the Henry barrel around to cover the horseman who had now come within a range of about a hundred yards. The light was good and the front sight stood out, big as a house, against the blue and brass of the coat which covered the breast of the jeering buck.

This shot would also be one for the Buffalo Hump, Sam was thinking, as he began to take up trigger slack slowly. The buck's pony kept veering about as it advanced. Sam wanted a dead sure shot so he was waiting. And then—as he pulled off—he was deafened by a cannon-like roar from the patch of quakers.

He saw the buck in the blue blouse plunge head foremost off his horse as though he had run into a rock wall. Nor did this buck roll like a bobcat when he hit the bunch grass. He lay motionless, there among the buttercups and the daisies, with the June sun shining straight down on his blue walkaheap coat.

That was the last shot fired that day in the battle of the Beaver Meadow. Sam's mates had not deserted him. Working their way cautiously down through the timber, as they had earlier advised Sam to do, they had taken up position in the quaker grove to the rear of Sam's rifle pit. At the crucial moment, when a bullet would count the most, Rocky Mountain Shorty had come into the fight with old Susy, his heavy calibre buffalo gun.

The death of the boaster who wore the blue coat of a soldier took the wire edge off the courage of the Sioux braves. While daylight lasted, they made no further attack. They hid in the willow brush. The two bucks, who had ridden out with the medicine man in the blue coat, whipped their ponies around, and fled into the timber west of the creek.

The afternoon sun felt hot as fire to Sam. He told himself that he would have traded his right arm for a long drink of cold creek water. But there was no way of obtaining a drink. His wound pained him. He knew that it required attention but he could not alone manœuvre a knife to cut out the arrow head. That must wait for Shorty and Tom Bear Mouth. They would not expose themselves just to save Sam a little suffering. They had already risked their hair by hanging around to save his bacon.

Sam had lost his slouch hat during the fight. He wrapped a dirty red bandana around his head to keep the sun from cooking his brains, also to prevent the sweat from running down into his shooting eye.

All he heard from his friends, after Shorty had let go with Susy, was a command from the old mountaineer to stay in his hole until dark came on.

"We'll try to get out then," said Shorty.

The long painful wait with a dead friend, in a narrow heated pit, gave Sam plenty of time for hard thought. The sense of guilt grew on him that he was to blame for this tragedy that had overtaken the expedition. If he hadn't discovered this spot of virgin trapping range, chances were that Buffalo Hump and his wife would be alive this minute over on the Wind River reservation with their Shoshone people.

It was a sort of new feeling to Sam Sling. He had always pursued an independent course of life since he had become an orphan in boyhood and taken to selling newspapers on the streets of St. Louis. When Rick, his older brother, persuaded him to enlist in the army after the close of the war, Sam had seized on it as a chance for adventure. The skeletonised regiments of horse and foot were being moved to western outposts to curb Indians, and to guard the new transcontinental railroad being pushed toward the Pacific.

Sam had served his hitch honourably enough, but, four years ago, he had taken his discharge and thrown in his lot with Rocky Mountain Shorty. Army rules and red tape irked his youthful impulsiveness. He wished to be free as the winds of the mountains. Rick, a professional soldier, had regretted Sam's scorn of service regulations, but they had parted friends.

Sam had learned about Indians from Shorty, and had discovered many things about them the hard way as he was being instructed this hot day in the looted beaver cache.

The beaver meadow had yielded rich returns for the winter catch, but a fortune in pelts, Sam told himself, was not worth a single hair of Buffalo Hump's scalp. He dared not reflect upon the fate of Night Star. She might be dead and scalped or a poor dishonoured captive in the hands of the Sioux raiders.

If Sam and his friends got out of these lonely mountains with hair on straight, they would receive no consolation or aid from the army. This entire country was barred against white civilians by federal regulations. The land had been lawfully turned over to Sioux control by treaty. The army had spread its forces along the reservation line to block eager white settlers from reaching Montana by way of the Bozeman Road through the Powder River country, or getting to the Black Hills mines by way of Hat Creek and the Cheyenne River.

Army patrols continually scouted the vast range, arresting and turning back trespassing settlers. Mountain men, like old Shorty and Sam, scorning army rules, took some pleasure in scoffing at army regulations. They knew the mountains and the deserts like the tracks of their own ponies. They risked their scalps, and ran their own chances for grubstakes in pelts.

But now the Sioux war party had the bulk of the winter's work, and, in addition, had dishonoured Tom Bear Mouth by scalping his brother-in-law. Bear Mouth would not set another beaver trap until he had restored his lost honour by avenging himself for the Hump's death and whatever fate had befallen his sister.

Sam knew that, by the code of the mountain men, he must follow Tom's lead. As would Shorty. There would be no more quick stakes, no more sprees when they "blowed in" with Canada Pete or at some other Wild West Oasis. They would kill or be killed by the Sioux before they resumed their free and easy life in the West.

The Sioux made no move to bring in the body of the warrior who wore the blue coat. Nor did they attempt a rescue of the wounded brave who had ridden the yellow pony. The long hours passed until darkness fell. In the first early gloom, Sam crept from his hole and sneaked back into the quakers where Shorty and Tom were waiting.

CHAPTER IV

Knowing the Indians feared to rove around in the darkness, having a superstitious belief that spirits of the dead then walked, Sam and his mates headed immediately for the high country where they had staked out the four pack horses. There was nothing to stay here for. The cabin had been turned down. There was no trace of the Night Star. They dared not even take a chance on burying Buffalo Hump.

Tom Bear Mouth had smeared his hair and face with soot and ashes from the charred ruins of the cabin. This indicated his grief over Buffalo Hump and Night Star, and his vow not to resume a normal life until he had attained vengeance or been killed trying.

They had lost all their supplies except for the spare ammunition in their packs, the clothing on their backs, and a few pelts they had taken during the ill-timed trapping trip to headwaters. They required these pelts to trade with Canada Pete for more ammunition and grub before they hit after the Sioux killers.

Pete's trading post was located a mile west of Cantonment Sparks, an army outpost on the Oregon Trail along the North Platte. Sam and Shorty had picked up some beaver traps from Pete the previous fall, when they shaped up for the trip into the Big Horns.

They forsook Sam's pet horse, Baldy, not daring to scout around in the darkness for the animal. With Shorty and Tom leading their saddle horses, and Sam following along, shirt cinched over his wounded side to strap up his wound, they put in rough hours of darkness climbing up through thick timber, and across old fire-burns where downed timber studded the earth. Toward daybreak, they found the pack horses. They paused only to eat a breakfast of jerked venison, washed down with water from a spring.

They crossed over the divide through a rocky, snow-studded

pass where slick rocks hid the hoof marks left by their horses.

They knew that they were now on the East slope of the Big Horns. All these small streams, fed by snowbanks and icy lakes, cut down through steep canyons, heading in a generally eastward course toward Powder River which ran many miles on beyond the mountains. Since the Sioux were horsemen, and hated footwork, the three trappers worked their way down a canyon afoot, choosing the roughest going over rocks, at times walking through icy snow water to hide tracks. They worked their stumbling pack horses over steep pitches by main strength, and Sam apologised for his "awkwardness." For his left side had stiffened up. He could not perform an expert share of the hard work with his usual deftness.

"Come daylight," Shorty panted once, when they were resting after working the string of horses down a neck-breaking fall of rock, "we'll look at that ar'er head. Right now, can't light a fire to work a knife. Chances are Injuns ain't out none in the dark. But we just can't take chances."

Dawn found them hidden out below steep canyon walls that rose for a thousand feet toward the blue sky. The roar of the stream dinned against their ears. Granite boulders, as large as houses, studded the banks of the stream. They led the pack stock and two saddle horses to the shadow of rocks where signs indicated wild animals had found shelter.

Bear Mouth, huddled in a ragged blanket, sat on guard while Shorty took his knife, rubbed his thumb along it to test its edge, and operated on Sam. With barbed fangs on the base, the arrow head could not be drawn out the way it entered. It was like a fish hook. Rather than waste time working it on through Sam's flesh, Shorty made a couple of quick slashes that Sam felt clear to his toes. He handed the bloody head to Sam. He was grinning.

"Part of the shaft on it. Leetle paint marks show the buck what owned it. Some day it might tell you who he was."

"He had a bucking horse painted on his chest," grunted Sam. He was glad he could find something to talk about, for

Shorty's cutting had revived all the agony of his wound. "I think he was the chief. Figure I hit him but don't know how bad. But I'll put this thing in my pouch. Might help Tom to run down one of the bunch that kilt Hump."

Shorty poulticed Sam's wound with a chaw of fresh tobacco and fluff from a beaver pelt, then strapped it up tightly with the tail of Sam's undershirt so Sam could travel easier. Sam tried not to flinch, but once or twice he ground out a curse.

"Try some of your singin'," Shorty advised. "Cracklin', Bub, what's a leetle old arr'er head amount to? Blackfeet put one smack dab in old Jim Bridger's back plumb over the kidneys. Jim's carried it for y'ars and y'ars. But this minute he's chipper as a squirrel and got married three times since and raised a couple of families. Take a chaw terbaccer, Bub. Rest easy. Our troubles are jest startin'."

When they broke from the mountains into open plains country, east of the range, the Sioux would be given a chance to overtake them, maybe make a kill if they caught the three trappers in some position where they couldn't make a good standoff.

That the hostiles were not sleeping away the daylight was now demonstrated. Tom Bear Mouth, vigilant in the mouth of the rock overhang that hid the horses, motioned with his soot-smeared head, then pointed silently with his chin, Indian fashion, to the rim of the high canyon wall above them. Sam and Shorty grasped their rifles, lay without speaking, eyes on that granite rim which appeared so near the blue sky of Wyoming.

They counted ten Indians passing along the top of the wall, riding in single file. The sunlight illuminated their painted bodies, the colours of their horses, even the eagle feathers they wore in their hair. Sam drew in his breath sharply when he noted that one warrior wore a blue army coat, that another was bestriding a yellow pony. But what most aroused his anger was that one of the Indians was leading his buckskin buffalo horse, Baldy.

"Now," growled Shorty, when the Sioux had disappeared, "they're ahead of us. From now on, we'll be dodgin' either Injuns or soldiers until we can hide out in Pete's place on the Platte."

When darkness fell they wearied of the difficult risky work of getting the string of horses down the canyon. When the canyon broadened out toward dawn, they decided it was now safe to mount up without risking a broken neck or leg. Tom Bear Mouth, usually silent because of his black grief, spoke briefly against it, saying that if light overtook them far out in open country, some distance from possible fighting cover, Sioux scouts might sight them. But the two white men had grown impatient. Sam's wound was edging his temper. Shorty was running short of tobacco. They knew they were at least sixty miles from Pete's post by the shortest route. They took to the horses at the first opportunity.

Shifting some of the packs, Sam mounted up on a barrel-headed roan pack cayuse. The animal was hard-mouthed, rough-gaited, far different from Baldy. That increased Sam's ire.

Shorty advised him to forget his troubles and invent a new verse for his song.

"Time to sing, Bub," he said, "is when you got lots of troubles."

CHAPTER V

Because of their impatience to reach safety along the Platte, they were caught by full daylight, far out from the mountains. They were traversing a rough country of red shale hills spotted with twisted cedars. There was not much cover. Far to the east, they could see the Black Hills as a hazy line along the eastern horizon. To the south lay the upper prong of the Platte where it made the big bend after the junction with Sweetwater. They had tied the three pack horses nose to tail in single file. Shorty brought up the rear, whipping on the pack stock with the braided end of a lash rope. Tom Bear Mouth rode in the lead, ever on the alert, hooded black eyes seeking Sioux sign.

The string of men and horses dropped through one narrow gap in a red rock wall. They came out into a shallow sage-brush valley. Across it loomed a steep rocky ridge running from north to south, and with the southern end dominated by a flat-topped butte.

Without a word, Tom Bear Mouth set his course toward the butte, and began to lash his tired pony down both sides with his quirt. Shorty was giving all get-out to the galloping pack stock. One pony lost a bale of beaver where canyon rocks had cut a lash rope. They did not pause to recover the pelts.

The sun was slanting down. It was now a murderous revealing glare. They were caught in a poor spot for a stand-off, on broken-down, tired horses. They didn't wish to desert their packs. They hoped that they could climb up on the butte, and barricade in the rocks before Sioux horsemen overtook them. As Shorty yelled, above the thunder of hoofs on the hardpan, he could smell Sioux Injun thick on the air as a buffalo dead three weeks.

With the wind blowing from the north, Sam stuck to that flank so that he would not be blinded by dust kicked up by the galloping horses. Every jump of his rough-riding pony sent a shaft of pain through his frame, but he knew that he must bear the pain and ride for his life.

True, he couldn't spot a Sioux sign in all the vast land which appeared warm and peaceful under the June sun. But his friends were wise to Indian ways through years of risky experience. They seemed to possess a sixth sense so far as hostiles were concerned.

Tom Bear Mouth, selecting the top of the butte as a natural fort, had headed straight toward it. Shorty, without objec-tion had followed Tom's lead.

In this rolling country where mountains gave way to the Great Plains, the sagebrush grew high and rough. Sam felt it brush his moccasins as his pony galloped ahead. Prairie dogs were chattering at their burrows throughout the warm valley. He hoped, fleetingly, that his clumsy, barefooted horse wouldn't stumble and fall over one of these dog holes.

Sam was not certain just where to keep an eye peeled for the Sioux attack. All he knew for certain was that the war party had ridden ahead of the trappers as the latter hid in the mountain canyon. He did know that the Sioux were crafty, highly skilled in war tactics, being acclaimed by military men as the finest natural cavalry that the world had seen. They might hit from either flank, from the front, or come dashing in from the rear.

A favourite war method of red raiders was to scatter a party—as Sam's outfit was now strung out—then dash in and cut off the leader or the men who brought up the rear. Or—if a man ventured too far out on the flank—they would cut in between him and the main party. Where the ground was hard and not dangerous for horses, the Sioux excelled in war.

The sagebrush grew thick down here below the rocky ridge, but sagebrush was not thick enough to turn aside war arrows or slugs fired from old muskets. Nor would it break up a rush of war ponies.

Tom Bear Mouth had selected the top of the butte as the nearest life-saving cover, and now was riding his pony down to a whisper to reach that position.

These horses were tired and hungry from the long journey down from the high mountain country. They had found short grazing during the various hideout camps, for they could not be hobbled and turned out to hunt grass. All these horses were of the Indian breed, and not one had tasted oats or corn in his life. They had, for the past few weeks, grown pot-bellied and soft on the lush green grass of springtime mountain meadows.

The frenzied speed to which they were now forced began to tell on the ponies. Sweat stood on their ribs and flanks like soap lather. Sam felt the faltering beneath him of his hard-running mount. If the pony gave up, Sam knew he would be left alone in the sagebrush to fight for his life.

Hanging to the bitter dust of the rear, Shorty gave his full attention to the pack horses. He trusted his comrades to keep an eye open for Indians. Shorty had lost one bale of beaver pelts on this run. He was a grim old realist. He would not give further tribute to the Sioux without a fight.

The sides of the butte were steep. Sam understood well enough that the stern test would come when the horses must be forced to climb its peak. He could see that it was not inaccessible. It was threaded with the narrow slanting trails worn through the grass during long centuries by pasturing herds of buffalo and other wild game. These angling trails would offer access to the top of the butte.

But wild game climbed or descended steep trails at a leisurely pace unless pursued by natural enemies. If the Sioux struck before Tom Bear Mouth rode out on the butte mesa, the horses would be forced to exert all the strength and heart they possessed to climb the steep slope.

A mountain man seldom jumped blindly into a fight with Indians. He lived to a green old age, if he was lucky, by planning ahead his tactics and strategems. The two white men, yielding to impatience, their desire to hurry, had forced themselves into a trap which might close at any moment. Sam Sling, up in the timber, through impulsiveness, had shown plenty of white bravery which would have amounted to nothing at all if Shorty and Tom hadn't risked their own hair to extricate him from the beaver cache.

Sam was quite well aware of all this as his horse bore him through the brush. He had determined that he owed a large debt to his two friends, even to the scalped Hump and the missing Night Star. He planned his further course of action with that in mind. He was young, and to him the sweet June breeze, and the sun pouring down on this wild, free western world, were precious. Life meant far more to young Sam Sling than to old Shorty or to grieving Tom Bear Mouth.

The infantry didn't train its soldiers as horsemen. But Sam had picked up all the tricks of a rider in the four years he had ridden the mountain country with Shorty. He figured he was jockey enough to whip his horse to a white lather, outride Tom to the top of the butte. There he'd be in the rocks and protecting himself with a magazine rifle.

Shorty would hang to the bales of pelts while he could. The loss of his entire outfit to the hated Sioux, even if he thereby saved his hair, would be as great a disgrace to the mountain man as the murder of Buffalo Hump had been to Tom Bear Mouth.

The unshod hoofs boomed on the hard earth. The wolfish yelp of a Sioux scout, even near at hand, could not have been heard by the three gallopers. Now and then Sam hung his chin on his shoulder for a look over the back trail. But he had long since decided that the Sioux would not be coming from that direction.

More likely they would be hidden on some flank waiting for the trappers to come to them. Laughing—as Indians often laughed—at the foolishness of the pale-faces.

Shorty's gun, old Susy, carried a powerful kick. But Susy was, after all, a single-shot rifle. If Shorty fell back to fight a rearguard action. He would get in one lick, kill but one warrior before they rode him down.

Sam knew that Shorty was stubborn. He would not easily give up his post of honour in the rearguard. But his legs were somewhat stiff with age. His heart and lungs had no longer the vitality of youth. Shorty would require all his power— like one of the pack horses—to climb to the top of the butte.

Even before the Sioux launched the flank attack, Sam turned his pony inward toward Shorty and the string of galloping pack ponies.

The warriors of the Sioux came tearing down at an angle from the crest of the long bare ridge which was dominated by the butte. They had hidden up there, waiting for the critical moment to arrive when they could most easily cut the white men away from cover, catch them strung out and off balance, and crush them in a wild charge.

The Sioux tore in from Sam's flank as Tom struck the first rocky pitch at the butte's base. The rolling dust hid the line of attack from Shorty's view except for momentary glimpses in the eddying haze. Shorty was yelling madly, wearing out his rope on the last pack horse in the string.

With crafty eye, Tom had selected the slanting trail that promised the easiest grade for running horses to the top of the butte. It would be a cruel climb of at least a hundred paces, but there was a chance of getting to cover if the Sioux could be brushed off in their first rush.

Riding in, Sam bent to the side and whipped up Shorty's mount. The mountain man, feeling his steed's sudden frightened gain in speed, swung in his saddle with a yell. He was staring into Sam's grimly set face. Shorty made a movement as though to halt his horse. But Sam quirted the old man's horse vigorously down the hind legs. Shorty, without time to pull back on bridle reins, was carried headlong across a narrow dry wash, filled with brush and rocks, in the wake of the clattering pack string.

The line of horses was crowding up the trail close on the heels of Tom Bear Mouth. Whatever had been Shorty's plan for the final round of his fight, Sam had driven him to where he could not pause until he had reached cover.

While Tom and Shorty and the laden horses puffed and sweltered their way up the side of the butte, dislodging rocks that crashed down through the brush and sparse growth of cedar, Sam opened his rearguard action.

He jumped his pony into the clear, away from the billowing dust that was bitter with alkali. He swept across the narrow wash at an angle, chose a broken pile of rocks that would temporarily serve as a rude barricade. As his pony floundered past the rocks, Sam swung to the ground. He lit, almost on the run, flung his body back of his shelter, and rammed the Henry stock to his shoulder.

Only by split seconds had Tom Bear Mouth won the wild race for the foot of the butte. But the Sioux had expected that they could ride in and pick off men and horses straggling up the steep trail. They had not expected that one pale-face would dismount to face them.

B.S.—2

The Sioux came in on the jump, flattened out along the backs of their hard-running little ponies. Expecting to cut off the three trappers, one by one, as they sought to climb the peak, the warriors were confused now by Sam's sudden change of plan. It was one thing to cut a man off a climbing horse, another to ride a pony straight up to the smoking black muzzle of a magazine rifle.

The Sioux didn't like it. They came fanning across the dry wash in a rolling haze of dust, but Singin' Sam was cutting the haze with a string of bullets. Above the barking roll of his Henry, he heard the howls of the red riders, the scuffling of the unshod hoofs of the wiry war ponies as the shaggy beasts slid down the steep side of the wash, then scrambled up the slope commanded by Sam.

Sam killed the first warrior who rode to his pile of rocks. He shot him through the middle, and the Sioux took a kicking headlong dive into the gravel of the wash.

"Wagh!" Sam roared, counting coup. "Wagh! The Sioux are squaws!"

One dead man proved enough for the moment. The raiders swerved away from the long hair's deadly gun that killed at a mile. Their war arrows rattled harmlessly off Sam's rocky barricade. They turned southward, riding so that they hung low from their ponies on the side away from Sam. He held his lead. He wasn't in this tight spot to shoot down horses.

Nor did he intend to hang around this patch of rocky cover while Sioux scouts, dismounting, slipped back to take him from the rear. He jumped up and began to climb the hill at an angle, quartering toward the south so that he could keep an eye on the Indians. In this rolling land, they could hide out almost instantly like rattlesnakes.

He was halfway up the hill and going at a dog trot around its face when he heard the shout of Rocky Mountain Shorty from the crest.

"Come on up! We got a hide-out! Everything fine 'ceptin' one pony with an ar' head in its rump!"

CHAPTER VI

But Sam yelled in answer that he aimed to scout out the Sioux hiding places before he rejoined. Shorty angrily disagreed, shouting in his high-pitched squawky voice, "No more of this white brave stuff! Why, up here we can stand off the hull Sioux nation!"

Sam persisted stubbornly in his scouting plan. He wished to spot the chief who rode the yellow pony if the man was still alive. Last time he had seen him go crawling for cover up in the beaver meadow. There was also the mystery of the bugle. And what about the Night Star? It was possible the woman was nearby, held captive by this war party.

Of course, Sam was not sure that the Sioux he had just fought were the men he had faced up in the mountains. The encounter on the bank of the dry wash had been too brief, too hazed up with dust and powdersmoke to give a man time for any sort of identification. About all he knew, anyway, was that the chief had a bucking horse painted on his breast, and that the hostiles also possessed the blue blouse of a soldier, now decorated with a bullet hole by Shorty's old Susy gun.

The sun blazed down on Sam's sweaty back, for buckskin was hot down here in June in the foothills. He meditated on jerking off the dirty, clinging hunting shirt, but his bare skin would draw clouds of buffalo gnats and that would irritate a man far more than the stiffness of his wounded side.

If they had patched up that chief and brought him along for this party, Sam figured he might get one long-range shot at the painted devil. That would be some skin back for the murdered Hump.

He came around the southern end of the long ridge, jogging along a narrow ledge above a shiny sheer wall of hot red rock. From this headland, perhaps fifty feet below the top mesa where Shorty and Tom were holed up, Sam took in a vast panorama.

To the east of the peak a long shallow valley ran from north to south; then on across it, a quarter-mile, another rocky divide reared its saw-toothed hump.

The valley was rough, and the rocks and treacherous prairie-dog holes of its floor were hidden by stands of giant grey sagebrush.

The heat, and the bitter smoke of burnt powder, had built up a powerful thirst in Sam's throat. The valley looked dry as the Red Desert. He had quit his pony, and the animal had stampeded, carrying away his water bottle. Shorty and Tom had enough water up on the peak to see them through the day, but Sam figured he was in for a dry session so long as the Sioux hid out around the foot of his ridge.

Some of them were smart enough to figure out Sam's gun range, for he saw three of the painted horsemen to the west of his position. They were not within killing distance. But they were near enough so that he made out the flash of a blue coat in the sun on the warrior who topped a yellow pony. One of the three was heavily blanketed. The thought came to Sam that this might be the missing Night Star, a captive held here to witness the wiping out of the two whites and her brother.

The wearer of the blue coat was apparently a chief, for he carried a long lance with eagle feathers dangling from its tip. With this, he was signalling to his men. The main body of warriors had taken to cover. They had hidden their ponies in some coulee concealed from Sam. They might be under observation of Shorty and Tom. Wherever they might be, Sam knew they were busy as ants, planning the most expeditious way of taking three scalps.

Alone here on this ledge, well aware that crafty Sioux might come boiling out from some concealed trail up the side of the slope, Sam felt no particular fear. If a man took time out to be afraid, he generally wound up with a bloody bald head. Best way to outwit the Sioux was to keep busy. Sam was busy now as a thin dog with a bad case of fleas. He squirmed around the nose of the ledge and dropped off the point, falling ten feet straight down into springy sagebush. One instant he had been under the eyes of the chief who rode the yellow horse. The next, he was as well concealed as any of the chief's followers.

The moment he hit his sagebrush mattress, Sam balled up arms and legs and forced his way through spiky branches to the ground. Beneath the cover of the sage was a cool world concealed from the killing rays of the western sun. Here the grass grew green and tender. The earth was damp. All around Sam were the dainty trails of the tiny field mice and the chipmunks. Prairie-dogs, those loud chatterers, never built their homes in the sagebrush.

When he had crawled at least ten feet from where he had landed, Sam chose a patch of inky shadow. He snaked into it, and hid there, listening to every tiny sound that reached his ears. Striving to select that mere whisper of sound which might warn of an Indian trailing his bare body through the grass.

But here within the giant grey sagebrush jungle was a cavern of silence; that peculiar silence of the Great Plains which seems to ring like a distant silvery bell in a man's ears. Sam could not even hear the rustle of the spring breeze in the leafy tops of the tall grey bushes.

Once Sam had satisfied himself that no painted warrior was nearby, he began a crawling course to the left, working his way slowly around the base of the butte. The ground rose gently. The brush began to thin out. Sam began encountering large rocks that had rolled down the slope of the peak.

One rock which Sam judged was the size of a small cabin barred his way. Thick brush grew all around it. Rather than snake around it, Sam began climbing over the rock. It felt hot as an oven, for it had been exposed to the merciless beat of the sun. Sam flattened out for an instant, flinching as his sore ribs touched hard rock. The sweat began seeping down into his narrowed eyes from his hair. He had taken off his red bandanna head scarf when he entered the brush, fearing the colour would attract the keen eyes of hostile scouts.

After he had blinked the salt sting from his eyes, he cautiously raised his head for another look around. As the top of the rock rose slightly above the sagebrush he discovered that he was high enough to scout out the long valley east of the peak.

What he saw a half-mile northward up the valley amazed Sam. Perhaps it also accounted for the silence of the Sioux and explained why they had not more hotly pursued him. A dusty wagon train was rumbling slowly along the valley. The vehicles would pass Sam's front if he remained long enough on his hot rock.

He counted seven wagons in the string, all drawn by mule teams. Then, a quarter-mile ahead of the train, and proceeding at a brisk pace toward him, Sam saw a light army ambulance drawn by a team of mules. He decided that the vehicle had gone ahead to escape the stifling dust raised by the wheels of the train and the hoofs of trudging mules.

Sam knew these light, canvas-covered ambulances were as often used by the army for hauling sound men through the fenceless West as for the sick and wounded. A team of mules could pull an ambulance at a brisk pace. On hot days, the canvas sides could be rolled up to admit the breeze, or in wintry weather, as tightly buttoned down to bar out the snow and cold.

Horsemen flanked the main train, holding their mounts to the slow pace set by the work teams.

Sam squinted his sun-dazzled eyes and growled under his breath. Some of those riders were not civilians. He could make out the heavy blue shirts and pants with which the army clothed its soldiers even in baking summer weather.

Here, where the three trappers had hoped to shake off the Sioux and strike for the Platte with the few pelts they had saved, the army barred the trail. If Sam and his friends were arrested on this Indian land, undoubtedly they would be relieved of their furs if worse did not happen to them.

The only hope of escape for the trappers was to hide on the butte, wait for the train to vanish, then take chances with the Sioux on getting to the Platte.

Sam knew that, even with a scalping knife point in the small of his back, old Shorty would not have called on the army for rescue. His friends, high up on the peak, had undoubtedly spotted the rolling dust of the train long before he squirmed up on his rock.

Since he was not under immediate threat, Sam decided to crouch here and endure the heat until the ambulance and the seven wagons, with attending soldiers, had passed.

It was odd, he ruminated, that this wagon train had come so far north into Sioux territory. He decided that the surrounding troopers indicated that some foolheaded party of emigrants had made a break for the north, been overtaken and put under arrest by an army patrol, and forced to swing around for the long roll back to the Platte.

The thought did not bother Sam, since he had little more time for wagon trains than for soldiers. These noisy emigrants frightened or wasted the game. They carelessly set fire to prairie grass, burning off good winter feed for the buffalo and antelope. They quite often got into a row with Indians that sent angry warriors blazing across the frontier eager for any white scalp they encountered. Most of the time, a mountain man knew which Indians he could trust, but greenhorn emigrants spiked the game for many a mountaineer and sent him to an untimely grave.

So Sam lay at ease, closely watching the approaching train, until, from the top of the ridge across the valley, he caught a flash of light from the corner of his eye. Instantly he was all attention. He set his eyes on the ridge and waited. The flash of light came again. He knew then that Sioux were over there, hidden on the ridge, using small hand mirrors to flash signals to braves hidden out near Sam.

Since he was quite sure they had not yet cut his trail, he decided the Sioux had scouted the train for hours and, with savage craft, had laid a trap for it.

Seven wagons would be difficult to capture. But that ambulance, so far in the lead, would be easily cut off. The soldiers, Sam thought, were fools not to call it back once they had seen the Indian mirror signals. He waited for some sign that would indicate the men with the train had spotted the savages' signals.

But the seven wagons, each drawn by four mules, came on at a leisurely pace. The ambulance, drawing farther ahead, was now not far to Sam's front. The wagoners and guards had either not picked up the signals or, in ignorance, had disregarded these indications of danger.

Sam knew that if he flipped up the Henry and let go with a string of shots, he would spread such an alarm that he'd break up any Indian trap.

Or he could fire off his Colt hand gun, warning the troopers of enemy in sight. But once he raised smoke and noise, he stood a good chance of losing his hair to some nearby Sioux. Or—if he escaped with his life—being put under arrest by the army. He might draw Tom and Shorty into the fight, cause them to lose their pelts, and break up any immediate plan of running down the killers of the Hump and Night Star.

It was not easy for Sam to decide to let the soldiers and the train roll into the Indian trap, or to see the careless ambulance get cut off. After all, he had worn army blue, and some of these indifferent guards might be men he had served with. It was not beyond the realm of possibility that his brother or his friends, Spike Dillon and Jimmy Kerry, were with the wagon train.

His old regiment was still stationed in Wyoming Territory. Companies had been shifted north to the treaty line since pressure had ended along the transcontinental railroad line. It was not easy to crouch here in the sun on a bare rock and unfeelingly watch a train of white soldiers and civilians rumble into the clutch of the Sioux.

But he believed that he owed a deep debt to Tom Bear Mouth and old Shorty. They would not approve of any move by Sam which might break up their plans for revenge.

They had not blamed him for luring them into the Big Horns, but it would be against the mountain code to make any rash move that would throw them into the power of the army.

Sam began to wonder just what form the Sioux trap would take. Whooping Indians might dash from that ridge across the valley on their ponies. The wagon train would halt hastily, circle around into a corral for fighting. While that move was being made, while wagoners and guards were vastly confused and excited, another force of Indians could dash in and cut between the ambulance and the main train. The mule team would be stampeded into a crazed runaway. The ambulance would be upset by some rock striking wildly spinning wheels. Then triumphant Sioux would canter off with the dripping scalps of whoever happened to be inside the ambulance, and whatever loot could be discovered in the vehicle.

Not that the Sioux cared much for stuff that pony soldiers valued. They would dare a company of infantry to get a gun, but they'd dump out valuable white flour on the prairie just to get the sacks. Indian squaws fashioned many glamorous garments from flour sacks. It wasn't likely the ambulance was carrying a load of flour, but Indians would as carelessly dispose of a case of precious medicine supplies.

CHAPTER VII

The ambulance was not far distant from Sam up the valley, and coming toward him at a smart pace. The mules were trotting along, but he saw that they were tossing their long-eared heads nervously. Now and then he heard the snap of the driver's whip and the loud curses with which the man sought to quiet his team.

Mules quite often became nervous when around wild Indians. Somehow, Sam knew, they held the same distaste for the red men that their white masters did. The Indians, for their

B.S.—2*

part, disliked mules. If they caught them, they killed them and roasted the flesh over their fires for a big feed. They seldom attempted to ride or pack the long ears so favoured by the pony soldiers for carrying food and ammunition.

Sam became so interested watching the approaching mule team and waiting for flickers of light from the opposite ridge that he inched to the edge of his rock. He had lain there for several moments when he discovered that, unwittingly, he had ventured into a portion of the Indian trap.

Directly beneath the overhang of his rock, a naked warrior crouched. The man was flat on his belly. He was so intent on watching the approaching train that he had not heard or seen the white man above him on the rock.

Nor would Sam have found the Sioux if he had not been drawn to the rock's edge by his interest in what was about to happen.

The rock was hot enough to fry an egg, but Sam froze. His body turned cold as ice for an instant. His first blinding thought was that the clever Sioux had forced him to reveal his position. Warriors might be crouching all around in the brush grinning balefully as they drew their skinning knives and made ready to jump this bold singer who had scorned them as squaws.

Then Sam relaxed. But only slightly. He was undiscovered for the moment. The warrior, crouching in the shade of the rock, gave no indication that he knew Sam was poised above him.

Sam took his sweaty hand grip off the Henry. The rifle would be unwieldy in a hand-to-hand fight if one broke out. Rather, he would rely on knife and Colt gun. He decided that he would drop off the top of the rock, land astride the Indian, and bury his knife to the hilt between the brave's shoulder blades.

Then he decided against that style of attack. He must make a silent kill if he hoped to get out of this tight alive. A knife in the back seldom resulted in silent loss of life. He had seen a man jump up and run a dozen yards with a knife sticking from his back. If he reached higher and got to the Indian's throat, the man would thrash around in the brush like a buffalo bull bogged in the mud while the blood gushed from his severed throat. But most of the time Sam knew, if a man was hit hard in the right spot on the head, he sprawled out with instant paralysis of mind and muscle. He could slide off his rock easily enough. But he must reach the Indian and strike an unerring blow before the warrior had time to yell an alarm.

Sam was just pulling up his legs and nerving himself for a drop from the rock when the Indian horsemen struck from across the valley. A dozen wild riders spurted down from the rocks and cedars of the opposite ridge. They sounded like a pack of hungry wolves as they drove straight toward the train.

Dust rose like smoke, and Sam heard the high shouts of wagoners, and the crackle of gunfire as the seven wagons rumbled around to form a corral.

Obscured by the golden haze, Sioux riders split off and made for the ambulance. Their yells alarmed the mules. The team, straightening out in the traces, stampeded off to the side, galloping toward the sagebrush-covered hill where Sam crouched above the Indian. This then was the Sioux plan. These warriors, hiding out, would rush in afoot, stab and kill once their mounted mates had headed the mule team into the sagebrush. Before help could come from the train, the ambulance driver and any passengers in the vehicle would be scalped and dead.

Sam saw the muscles tighten like rope in the brown back of the Sioux who lay at the base of his rock. The frightened mules were heading straight toward him. They were not fifty yards distant. He could see the blue-clad driver tense in the seat, boot on the brake, hands tight on the taut reins.

The man was so near that Sam could even make out his fear-distorted face, a face he had grown to hate four years before at Ford Fred Steele. It was Corporal Bootle, who had driven young Sam from the army with his envy and arrogance. Bootle was about to lose what hair he still possessed to the Indians that the army was protecting from whites like Sam.

Sam grinned balefully at the thought of how much these

war whoops required protection. If Bootle had not been such a fat-headed fool, he would have swung his mules when the Indians made their first rush, and tried to outrun them back to the main train. Down here, with his kicking mules tangled up in the brush, with his ambulance halted, even upset, Bootle would not have a chance.

Singin' Sam Sling hated Corporal Bootle very heartily. Of all the soldiers he had encountered, Bootle would have won his vote for booby prize. But when Sam Sling looked upon the puffy, terrified face of Bootle, he ground out a curse, jerked his six-gun, and dropped off the top of his rock.

He hit the Sioux warrior so crushingly that he drew a grunt from the man. The man had time only for that grunt. For the moment Sam felt his knees against the earth on each side of the Sioux, and his crotch pressing down on the warrior's backbone, he hammered him back of the ear with the barrel of his Colt. A slight sound, and that was all. A steely *thuck* like a keen axe blade sinking into a sappy pine log. But that single blow was enough to cave in the Indian's skull where bone grew thin above the warrior's right ear.

Sam felt all the life go out of his victim as he sat astride the quivering body. He stayed a moment, finger on cocked gun hammer, waiting for another warrior to jump him. They hadn't heard. They were watching the runaway mules, licking their lips for the hot blood of Corporal Bootle. The ambulance struck a rock, lurched over, and upset. The mules began to kick and fight in the harness. Bootle, thrown clear, scrambled like a fat June bug toward the nearest cover.

And then, above the pounding of hoofs and the snap and rattle of iron and wood and leather being destroyed, Sam heard the clear scream of a woman in the very extremity of of fear. So Bootle had had a passenger in the ambulance. A white woman. Here, deep inside hostile territory. The runaway mules had brought her into the power of the merciless Sioux.

Sam Sling jumped off the body of the brave he had just killed. He went tearing down through the brush, six-gun

flaming as he flung lead into the front of the Sioux riders,
as they rushed in to capture the ambulance, the mules, and
Bootle and his passenger.

The sudden appearance of the lanky mountaineer in dirty
flapping buckskins emerging from tall sagebrush on the high
slope, behind a flaming six-gun, amazed the charging warriors. Sam's bullets were flying wild. He wasn't hitting any
live targets, for he was shooting to win time to reach the
wrecked ambulance.

"Wagh!" whooped the leading buck, a sinewy warrior
who had striped his face with green and black war paint.
"Wagh!" And he broke away to the flank less than ten
yards from the ambulance.

The woman continued to scream as Sam galloped in. The
two mules were rearing and bucking, striving to kick their
way free of entangling harness. Two warriors, pressing closely
behind their leader and half blinded by the dust kicked up by
pony hoofs reached the ambulance ahead of Sam. But, inad-
vertently, they arrived just as one of the mules broke an outside trace and whirled around to back away from his team
mate. The sight and smell of the Indians drove the two mules
entirely mad. The animal that had almost freed itself flung
out its hind legs, and with the unerring aim with which mules
are blessed, landed both hoofs squarely against the breast
of one of the Sioux war ponies.

Squealing, walling its eyes, the pony went back on its
haunches, almost hurling off its painted rider. The second
buck, laying back on the line of his war bridle, striving to
check his mount before he came in contact with the plunging
mules, came within Sam's line of aim as he neared the
ambulance.

Sam figured his gun had about run dry, but this was the
best target of the day, barring the brave up in the brush
whose skull he had broken. He let go. The Colt slug tore a
gaping hole through the bent back of the Sioux.

When the dead brave flopped off his mount, that broke up
the immediate fight around the ambulance. The war party,

that had fancied itself on the verge of taking pony soldier hair cheaply, scattered to the four directions of the compass.

The tough hickory tongue of the ambulance which had until now withstood vast strain, cracked like a fire cracker as Sam scrambled up and over the canvas side.

When the tongue broke off, the mules were finally released. They bolted deeper into the sagebrush, dragging with them remnants of harness and double-trees. The Sioux fighters, who had been in hiding, waiting for their mounted friends to drive the team into their trap rose up and began to snap whizzing war arrows at the mules. One animal went down, as full of quivering arrows as a pin cushion. But its mate somehow unhit, went on kicking and plunging on through the brush.

Sam, finding a canvas curtain rolled up, thrust his long legs into the ambulance, intending to find cover inside the vehicle. Given a couple of split seconds, he figured he'd have time to unload the hot, smoke-blackened Colt.

Another screech of fear from the woman he had saved deafened him. He turned his head and found himself staring down into a smudged face surmounted by a tumbled wealth of shining chestnut hair. She had raised her head through the opening in the side of the ambulance.

A Sioux war arrow, flying wild, hissed past Sam's ear. He planted his left palm on top of the woman's head and gave a hearty push.

"Stay down!" he yelled. "Stay down!" And added, greatly irrated, "And quit screechin' like a hoot owl!"

He broke open his hand gun, raked shells from his belt, and began to reload. One empty shell was so hot it had jammed. Sam, who didn't wish to take his eyes off the enemy in the brush, cursed the shell. He jerked his skinning knife, got the edge of the blade beneath the rim of the shell, but the blade slipped free when he sought hurriedly to pry out the shell. He dropped the knife, decided he'd not waste time attempting to extract the empty. But when he attempted to snap back the cylinder, the contrary rim blocked the action.

Given a few moments of time, Sam could easily enough have cleared the cylinder and reloaded the gun.

But here in a hot and panicky fight, with war arrows whirring through the air, and crazily yelling Sioux trying to kill a bucking mule, Sam wasn't able to think or move calmly. He knew that he was caught without a weapon for the defence of the woman and himself unless he could recover the knife which he had dropped. He wished that he hadn't laid the old Henry down on that hot rock.

He couldn't look in all directions at once, and he had lost sight of the corraled wagon train and the Sioux riders. He was watching the Sioux who had jumped from the brush to grab the stampeding mules. He saw the kicking body of the animal that had been filled with arrows. And then he saw a Sioux buck make the mistake of attempting to seize the trailing bridle rein of the wild-eyed mule that was still on its feet.

The buck jumped like a jack rabbit toward the mule's head. He got a close grip on the bridle headstall. The mule reared back, letting out a strangled bawl, whipped the buck off his moccasins and so high into the air that his breech clout floated like a flag in the Wyoming breeze.

The mule began to rear back through the brush, shaking its head madly, striving to free itself of the clinging weight of the Indian. The buck appeared stubborn. He would not let go of the headstall.

Then, with dreadful suddenness, the Indian dropped the bridle rein. His paint-streaked body went limp as a dish rag. He flopped down over the top of a tall sagebrush and hung there, feebly kicking his legs. As he fell, from the top of the butte came the boom of a gun.

Sam knew that at last Rocky Mountain Shorty had bought into the fight with old Susy. He had shot the Indian off the mule's head. But with black powder ammunition of slow velocity, and firing at long range, a man was apt to drop dead before the sound of the gun's report reached an observer's ears.

In the dust and smoke, Sam counted three Sioux afoot in

the brush. When they saw their friend die quickly, when they heard the dull roar of old Susy, they all dived back into cover.

Sam looked around for Corporal Bootle, but couldn't spot where the fat driver had taken to cover. Now he would find time to reload his contrary gun. But as he bent and began to fumble around inside the ambulance for the knife he had dropped, the stock of another hand gun was shoved into his hot hand.

"Here's one fresh loaded," the woman quavered. "I was saving it for myself!"

CHAPTER VIII

Sam looked down into her dirty face. He thought she would probably look younger and prettier if she could find time to wash herself.

"Tarnation," he snarled, angry that she hadn't passed him the gun sooner. "Coulda took some more Injun hair if you hadn't been so worrit about yourself!"

Greenhorns always took stock in tall stories about the women saving the last bullets for themselves in an Indian fight. Of course, if the men were captured, quite likely they'd roast over a slow fire. But Indians seldom killed any young or pretty women they captured. They carried them off to camp and trained them to skin buffalo, pack wood and water, and help out their squaws. Sometimes they married them, although a lot of Indians didn't think fragile white women rated as squaws.

"I couldn't have stood it," the girl half-sobbed, "if those fiends had caught me."

"Shoulda figured on that when you headed up the Bozeman Road to Montany."

"But we were going west to the Wind River country. To the Sweetwater mines."

Sam opened his eyes wide in amazement. "You're a good sixty miles off that road," he finally pointed out. Then he decided that she was lying to him and that angered him. "Fools like you," he growled savagely, "would do 'most anything to pick up some of those gold nuggets in the Black Hills or Montana." For he had encountered gold-crazed newcomers to the West who actually believed they could pick gold off the surface of the ground like a chicken picking up grains of feed.

His angry voice acted on the girl like a cold drink of water. It stirred her wrath and drove the fog of terror from her mind. She pushed up at his side, and her eyes were now almost on a level with Sam's. He saw that she was a tall and well developed girl. She was wearing some sort of a blue gown of light fabric. Sam now turned his head and looked up the long valley toward the train.

The wagons still stood in a rough circular corral. He heard guns popping now and then like distant firecrackers at occasional Sioux horsemen who appeared on the eastern ridge. But the main fight had been beaten off.

Toward the wrecked ambulance came a bunch of galloping horsemen. They wore the army blue. Several were riding on mules. At last the army had sent a rescue party out.

"About time," Sam grunted. "Danged coffee coolers!" He began to look around the immediate surroundings. "Where's Bootle?" he asked.

"Bootle?" she wanted to know.

"That fat fool who was driving you."

"Oh—I thought you meant the other soldier. The lieutenant down here inside the ambulance."

Sam's black brows went up. "Tarnation," he gasped, "you still got another soldier in this heap?"

"Look," she said, pointing downward.

Sam's eyes followed the motion of her arm. He found himself staring down into the interior of the ambulance. The flaring skirt of the girl's gown half hid the sprawled form of a man in a blue uniform. But Sam made out the yellow colour of stripes on pants and bars on shoulder straps.

"A shavetail," he said. "A danged cavalry lieutenant. What's he doin' in here? Why isn't he out with the rest of those boys?" And he gestured toward the oncoming knot of mounted men.

She had the grace to blush. "His name's Prime. Lieutenant Nat Prime. He's been quite polite since his men stopped our train. This morning he decided the ambulance should go ahead to stay out of the dust. And he'd ride with me so that he'd be on hand if we got into any trouble."

"He was a lot of help," Sam laughed.

"Anyway, when your gun played out, I handed you his six-shooter."

"My gun didn't play out."

"Well, something happened to it. You were fumbling around there, looking wild-eyed, using foul language something awful."

"And you were screeching your fool head off. No wonder I went plumb locoed and busted up my gun action. That's what happens to a man out here when he gets tangled up with fool-headed females. Just like Shorty says: only place fer women is in town. You can buy 'em a drink or so, dance and have a good time with 'em. But leave 'em behind when you hit the trail."

Before she was able to reply, soldiers came up on the gallop.

They were a nondescript-appearing outfit, in their dusty, baggy blue pants with the tops stuffed into heavy socks, their feet clad in broad-toed army issue brogans. The majority wore blue fatigue-caps. Their heavy blue shirts were grey with dust, and their broad red hairy faces were grimy with trail dirt and powder soot.

Sam lifted up the girl and swung her clear of the wrecked ambulance. Then he released his grip on her muscular body. She slid down the canvas side to the earth. He climbed out the opening and hastily set his moccasins on the ground. He was toting the lieutenant's six-gun at full cock, warily watching the soldiers. For he didn't know just what to expect from them.

The leader of the party, who had galloped up on a grey mule, hustled towards the girl and Sam. He was a sinewy sort of trooper, with a lank black moustache outlining his hard-set thin lips. He wore a cavalry style slouch hat cocked on the side of his narrow head, but Sam saw that the white chevrons and stripes of an infantry corporal decorated his shirt and breeches.

This amazed Sam, since the unconscious lieutenant inside the ambulance, the shavetail called Nat Prime by the girl, was apparently from the horse branch of the army. It struck him as strange that a pony soldier should be commanding a detail of walk-aheads.

But he forgot his surprise when he took another look at the approaching corporal. Four years had passed since the old days in Fort Fred Steele, but a man never forgot the friends with whom he had passed a few days in the guard-house after pay day.

"Dillon!" he cried joyfully. "Spike Dillon!" Sam stepped forward, right hand extended and opened. There was a wide grin on his face. "What are you doin', away up the Powder? And ridin' a jarhead mule?"

Spike Dillon stopped dead in his tracks as though he had been shot through the heart. His black eyes, as bright and hard-looking as bits of badland soft coal, flashed a glance past the girl toward Sam Sling.

"That voice," Spike said huskily. "I recognise it. But who are you behind all that hair and trail dust?"

These soldiers had come up so swiftly that many had not seen details of the fight around the wrecked ambulance. Some were carrying their long Springfield army rifles, the old .45-70 calibre single-shot guns of Civil War days, at full cock. They hadn't failed to note the long blue pistol held by Sam. They knew all about this latest model of the Colt, and had a powerful respect for its mighty kick.

"Now see here, boys," roared Sam Sling. "Don't go to shootin' me up, figurin' I'm a danged renegade that runs with

war whoops. Spike Dillon, here, knows me well. Many's the
time I helped to sober Spike up after a pay day. Why, down
at Fort Steele, onct I toted him out'n Chicago Jack's joint
after a card shark had clipped him over his head with a pistol. Spike—tell these coffee coolers to sorta stand at ease
while we line up on just what went on here."

Spike Dillon jerked his hard features into a black frown.
"Sling," he growled. He never offered to take Sam's welcom-
ing hand. "One of those Slings!" He stepped past the girl.
"What are you doin' away up here in Injun country?" There
was now deep suspicion in his harsh voice. He glanced hastily
about him. "Where's the lieutenant?" he went on. "And what
become of Corp'ral Bootle?"

Sam felt aggrieved that his man, whom he regarded as one
of his army bunkies, should meet him after four years with
hard eyes and harsh voice.   -   -

"Why Spike," he complained, "I reckon Bootle's layin'
around somewhere, maybe fainted or somethin' from his
Injun scare. That shavetail from the cavalry is all laid out
inside the ambulance. Me and this young woman—" He
nodded toward the girl.

Spike cut him off sharply "You're under arrest, Sling.
Better lay down that gun!"

"Now listen here, Spike," Sam began angrily, rage beginning to simmer. "I'll lay down this gun when I danged
please. The gal passed it to me when mine run dry. Them
Sioux woulda got our hair shore if she hadn't. That's what
happens when yuh depend fer any help from the danged
army. What did you boys take so much time fer when the
hostiles started yellin'? Did yuh have to stop and eat breakfast?" Sam was bearing straight down on Spike. "What's
come over you, anyway?" he roared. "Turnin' down an old
bunky this way."

Sam's anger failed to daunt Spike. The corporal called to
his men, "Keep him covered. If he tries to use that pistol,
open fire." Then Spike repeated to Sam, "You're under
arrest. Hand over your gun!"

"Spike," Sam said, between his teeth, "you haven't got enough men with you to get my gun! Any time you aim to try, cut loose your wolf!"

Spike, unafraid, held his ground. "For the last time," he said, "hand me that gun. Stock first."

"For the last time, Spike, come and get it."

They were not six feet apart. Spike carried a pistol in the holster on his cartridge belt. His blue-clad detail supported him, rifles held ready to open fire on Sam at the latter's first hostile move.

It was the girl who broke up the coming battle. She stepped between Sam and Corporal Dillon. Her blue eyes were stormy. "This man," she told Dillon, "just saved me from the Indians. Also your lieutenant who's sprawled out inside the ambulance, may be hurt bad. Why are you handling him as though he were a common criminal—a murderer? I handed him that gun which I took from your officer when he could not use it. To stop you men from a shameful killing, I'll take it away."

She swung on Sam, and held out her hand. He stood braced on his moccasins, breathing hard through his nostrils like a wind-broken racehorse. His thick black brows were drawn down over his smoky grey eyes in a frown. His gaunt jaws were set, his hairy chin thrust out like a saddle horn.

"If she jest touches him," one doughboy drawled to another, "she'll blister her finger."

"Use what horse sense you got," she said to Sam. "You can see you haven't any show against all these army guns. "Hand over that six-shooter and tell your story to the lieutenant when he comes out of his dreams. I'll back you up every inch of the way. If it hadn't been for you, we'd all be scalped this minute. Me, Lieutenant Prime, and that fat corcorporal who doesn't know the first thing about handling mules."

Her calm talk took the wire edge off Sam's wrath. After all, shooting it out against a dozen rifles would be just more of the white brave courage that Tom Bear Mouth had derided.

Sam smiled grimly, but he bowed and reversing the six-gun handed it over, stock first, to the girl. Instantly, she turned on Dillon.

"Now you're safe from him. He's afoot. He can't run off. Hadn't you better take care of your officer? Also see what happened to Corporal Bootle?" She tilted her nose and sniffed. "Since you were a trifle late to fight Indians, you can at least take care of your own men."

Spike's hard features turned red with fury. But he turned away and gave sharp orders to his men. They lifted the lieutenant from the ambulance, worked their way into the sagebrush where they found the groaning Bootle who had hidden behind a rock. One of the searchers also discovered the dead Indian with the cracked skull, and Sam's Henry rifle still resting on the rock.

A slug of cold water from a canteen revived Lieutenant Prime. He stood up, rather groggily, on his cavalry boots, rubbing a bump on his head as large as a sagehen egg. He was a tall, fair-haired young man, sporting a flowing cavalry-style moustache.

Prime's first concern was for the girl. "Miss Payne," he implored, "I don't know how to excuse myself for getting you into such danger. I never thought those accursed savages were so near." He turned on Bootle, paunchy and fat-faced, who stood on sagging legs supported by two grinning soldiers. "You," he said sternly, "who ever told you that you could drive mules? Letting that team run off at the first Indian yell! Why didn't you turn them back to the main train?"

"Now, Lieutenant," Bootle pleaded huskily, "I couldn't do a thing with those mules. They go crazy when they see or smell Injuns."

"A few days back," Prime answered tartly, "you had different ideas about mules. You classed yourself as an expert on mules before the board of review at Cantonment Sparks."

"But that was different, Lieutenant."

"Not much different. Another case of Indians frightening a man's mount."

"But he was riding a horse, not a mule."

Prime shrugged, turning to Dillon. "Corporal," he ordered, "have three of your men dismount. They will remain here and attempt to repair the ambulance. Bootle can stay with them. The rest of us will return to the wagon train and get under way."

Bootle almost wept. "Lieutenant, don't leave me here. Them Injuns may come back. I haven't got a gun."

"Pass him a rifle," said Prime. He bowed to the girl as a soldier led up a pony. "I hope I'm forgiven," he murmured.

"You should thank this man here in the buckskin for saving us," she told him. "I don't know where he came from. But he arrived at the critical moment."

Prime nodded, turned to Sam and thrust out his hand. "Sorry," he apologised. "I'm in your debt for the lives of Miss Payne and myself."

Sam grinned, shaking hands with him. "You're the first soldier in four years," he said, "who's treated me civil. That Spike Dillon there," he frowned, "he wanted to shoot me."

Prime turned on Spike, and the corporal growled, "I was just trying to arrest him, sir. That's our orders. Arrest all civilians found north of the treaty line without army passes. His name's Sling. Sam Sling. He's a mountain man. He hasn't explained yet what he's doin' up here."

"Sling." Prime scratched his head, flinched as his fingers touched the big bump. "You any relation to Sergeant Rick Sling?"

"My brother," said Sam.

Prime looked dubious, shook his head, narrowly regarding Sam. Then he sighed and went on. "I must place you under arrest as the corporal has explained. That's our orders from headquarters at Fort Fetterman. My name's Prime. I'm commanding this detail of mounted scouts from one of our outposts down on the Platte. If you'll just mount one of those ponies, we'll return to the train."

CHAPTER IX

Sam nodded and mounted up. He felt glad that they hadn't questioned him closely about his business up here. He knew that Tom and Shorty were undoubtedly still upon the peak, watching all that went on, doubtless cussing him heartily for getting involved in a fight with Indians and being captured by the army. He decided that if they questioned him again at the train, he'd swear that Indians had stolen some of his horses, and he'd followed them north to recover the stock. If they didn't accept that excuse, he would just shut up and let them take him to the river and shove him south of the line. Shorty and Tom would soon show up around Canada Pete Narbo's trading post. They'd get fixed up and hit the trail, hunting for the Night Star.

As he jogged back to the train, he chatted with the soldier who rode at his side. He wanted to know about his brother, and news of the old regiment. He was informed that the first battalion had been sent north from Steele in the early spring to help guard the treaty line. Headquarters had been established at Cantonment Sparks on the river. Several outposts had been laid out from which to watch trails which trespassing whites might take to the north to Montana or the Black Hills. These mounted scouts were from one of these outposts located ten miles north of Cantonment Sparks.

Sam had to laugh. "Mounted scouts." He shook his head. "Half of you ridin' mules. What's come over the old infantry anyway? And a hoss lieutenant to command you."

"Short on troops," his guard answered shortly. "Hard walkin' out here. So the army bought some Injun ponies and mules and mounted some of us up. That loot you met, he's from a regiment of hoss at Fort Laramie. Detailed on special duty to our outfit to instruct us in mounted scoutin' and the like."

"Tell him to keep his eyes open for Injuns usin' a lookin' glass to send signals," Sam suggested.

"He was inside the ambulance. That girl was keepin' him right busy. He's sweet on her."

"Miss Payne?"

"Her hull name is Jane Payne. She owns most of that wagon train. Five wagons. Loaded with flour and grocery goods, she says, intended for the Sweetwater mines. She's a cornfed from Missoury."

Sam could see Jane Payne riding ahead of the detail beside the lieutenant. Prime was bending from his McClellan saddle, very attentive to Jane. She was laughing. Out on the flank rode Spike Dillon. Sam's grin faded to a scowl when he spotted Spike.

"I'd like to catch him out in the sagebrush," he growled. "He's got pretty black eyes. But I'd make 'em a sight blacker. Turnin' down an old bunky. One that dragged him out of Chicago Jack's deadfall down at Fort Fred Steele."

"So you put in a hitch? What did you get? Bobtail?" the guard asked curiously.

Spike spat out angrily, "They gave me an honourable discharge. I put in a full hitch. I'd've resigned if it hadn't been for that fat Bootle. He was ridin' me. He hated my brother, Rick, who was first duty sarge in the company. Ready to take over top kick when old McNeal stepped out."

"So Rick Sling's your brother. Well, he did get made first when the battalions came north."

"Good. I'll see Rick when we get to Cantonment Sparks."

"You may see him but you may not find it good."

Sam frowned. "What do you mean by that?"

The soldier shrugged. "Ask your old bunky, Dillon," he suggested.

Sam tried to dig out more information but his guard shut up like a clam.

Sam saw that the main wagon train was approaching, four mules dragging each heavy canvas-covered vehicle while bearded skinners sat on the high seats handling the reins and the brakes. Several horsemen led the train. One, on a handsome black horse, halted the train as the detail came up, then cantered forward to meet the soldiers. Prime halted his detail and rode forward with Jane Payne to greet the rider.

Sam squinted his eyes against the settling dust and the sun glare. That rider looked almighty familiar in his high black boots, his fringed buckskin hunting shirt, his long black hair that curled from beneath a wide-brimmed hat of cream colour, creased down the middle. He saw the nattily garbed horseman bend gallantly in his saddle, and bow his head over Jane Payne's hand as she rode up beside him.

"Gah!" growled the soldier guard. "Kissin' her paw like a Frenchy. That Hacker's a devil with the women. Got some more along on this train that likes kisses."

"More?" snapped Sam. "You mean more than one white woman was fool enough to poke into war whoop territory."

The guard grinned. "Wait until you see the others. Sunset Liz and her two younger sisters, Dotty and Dolly."

"Sunset Liz. Why, I've heard tell of her. She run a big quick lunch joint onct in Cheyenne, when the town was boomin'." He saw that the rider, Hacker, had turned and was escorting Jane Payne and the lieutenant back to the train. The name of Hacker touched up a memory in his mind, of a smoky night in Fort Fred Steele and a fight in a card sharp's dive.

"Hacker," he said. "That's his last name. But he's more generally known as Chicago Jack. What's he doin' up here with a bunch of women in his train?"

"Hard to tell what he has up his sleeve. That Payne gal claims he hired out to show 'em a new trail to the mines on Sweetwater. She's got her guardeen along. An old pelican what calls himself Judge Barberry. They all swear they didn't know they was across the line. Say they had heard grass was short on the regular trail to South Pass and Miner's Delight, and they aimed to swing a leetle north and around the southern point of the Big Horns."

Sam swore. "Bah," he growled. "Chicago Jack knows this range well as I do. He's been up the Bozeman Road to

Montany. He wouldn't go so far wrong. No—he's got somethin' up his sleeve, all right."

Sam was given no opportunity to face Chicago Jack Hacker. For when the mounted scouts rejoined the main train, the caravan immediately resumed the long and tiresome return journey to Cantonment Sparks. Sam rode with the troopers but soon discovered that, although several had served with him, none would talk to him as a friend. This fired up Sam's anger. As he jogged along, he passed the time framing another verse to his buffalo song that he hoped would sting the pride of his former bunkies.

The lieutenant commanded a noon halt at a water hole but allowed no time for boiling coffee. Horses and mules were watered. Soldiers grumbled as they ate their cold rations, consisting mainly of hard tack and bacon previously fried at their breakfast mess fire.

With nearly sixty miles to travel to the Platte, the lieutenant hoped to make the return trip in three days. Ordinarily this would have proved a killing pace for slow-moving wagons, but fear hung over the expedition that the hovering Indians would gather reinforcements and launch a full-scale attack.

Sam watered the keg-headed pony with which he had been furnished, then picketed the animal on a forty-foot rope to nibble the scanty grass. He planted his broad back against a tall sagebrush, and between bites into a sandwich of greasy bacon and hard tack softened up by being soaked in water, he sang for the disgruntled soldiery.

"Oh—take me back to the buff'ler days,
When Injuns whooped in the prairie haze.
Doughboys were half mules, half men.
If they ever changed, Gawd knows when."

Spike Dillon arose from the knot of his blue-clad mates with a murderous look on his face. He stepped over to Sam, and glared down into Sam's wide open mouth.

"Shut up your bazoo," said Spike, "or I'll shut it for you."

Sam grinned and tossed aside the remnants of his lunch. He uncoiled his lanky body leisurely. He faced Spike, wiping bacon grease off his hands on the flapping outside seams of his buckskin pants.

"So you don't like my singing'," he jeered. "Well, here's another verse that might please you better."

He flung back his head and his twangy voice rose above the rustle of the wind in the sagebrush, and the confusion of the noon camp. Mule skinners, sitting in the shade of covered wagons, grinned and halted their eating to listen. At the head of the train, Lieutenant Nat Prime broke off his polite chatting with Miss Jane Payne, and hurried back to where his men were stationed with their horses.

> "Oh—take me back to the buff'ler days,
> When Injuns whooped in the prairie haze,
> Would fight right hard for a private's hair
> But passed up a corp'ril's, I do declare."

As Sam whined out the last word, Spike Dillon hit him. But Sam expected that. He rolled his head with the punch, taking a glancing blow on his lean cheek. He blocked Spike's furious charge with upflung left arm, then thrust back the angered corporal. Trained in rough and tumble fighting in many an army brawl, Spike saw immediately that Sam had lured him into a trap. He attempted hurriedly to get up his guard. But before he could push his left fist into Sam's grinning face, the mountain man stepped in, right fist sweeping up in an uppercut that popped off the point of Spike's chin.

Being a tough man, the corporal was not knocked out by the savage punch, but he reeled away from Sam, groggy in his boots, shaking his head madly to clear the fog from his brain.

Sam followed up mercilessly, swinging rights and lefts until his knuckles reddened with Spike's blood. He was cutting Spike's hard face to red rags, jarring him from belt to collar-button with punishing blows.

The corporal's fellow troopers, dropping hard tack and fat bacon, jumped up and crowded around the two battlers. Foremost in the group was Corporal Bootle, who had been picked up earlier when the train passed the wrecked ambulance.

Sam was enjoying himself hugely, taking out all his ire against the army on luckless Spike Dillon. Spike would think twice, he told himself, before he ever again turned down an old bunky who had once befriended him in a tight spot. He pressed in closer to his weaving target, eager to knock him out for a full count. Spike's eyes were swelling shut. But he was a game lad. He stayed on his legs, with guard up, although his knees were beginning to buckle.

"Pull that murderin' thief off Spike!" bawled Corporal Bootle, appealing to his muttering fellow soldiers. "He's tryin' to kill Spike! The dirty renegade!"

Spike pawed out blindly, seeking to close in and hang to Sam's body for a moment's breather. Sam padded around like a mountain lion in his soundless moccasins. Lightly, he brushed away Spike's wavering fists. He snapped a punch to Spike's paunch. As the corporal fell forward, Sam stepped in and straightened him up with a sock to the chin.

The corporal's knees broke. He went down in a heap, still conscious but so weakened that he could not stay on his feet and fight.

Bootle, calling on soldiers to help the corporal, had ventured within arm's reach of the grinning, bloody man he had called a renegade.

"Wah!" roared Sam, giving a war whoop. He reached out and grabbed Bootle by the slack of his collar. He twisted Bootle's shirt about his kneck so tightly that Bootle began to strangle and turn blue. Sam held him thus with his left hand. With opened right hand, he slapped Bootle, first on one fat cheek, and then the other.

"I'm gettin' even," Sam yelled, "for the mules you couldn't drive!"

Bootle opened his mouth in a choked squawk which Sam shut off with another open-handed slap.

But Sam was also keeping a wary eye on the remaining soldiers. They were crowding him closely. They were hot with wrath. A half-dozen hard men were there. Some were away from the halted train, holding a picket line against further Indian attacks.

Bootle's squalls and Sam's war whoops drew others to the fight. Bearded mule skinners hurried to the rear of the train where soldiers were circling around the battlers. Lieutenant Prime pushed impatiently past the grinning teamsters.

A woman thrust her head out the rear of one of the wagons. Her bright red hair gleamed in the sunlight.

"Loot" she cried out, in a husky but not unmusical voice, "what's all the big noise about?"

Prime shook his head angrily, never pausing to explain. But a huge mule skinner known as Red Dog, whose hair and beard matched the woman's flaming red hair, bawled out an invitation.

"Git your gals, Liz! Come on out! The doughboys is puttin' on a show!"

Sunset grinned and nodded. She called out loudly, "Gals, we're missin' somethin'!"

Liz swung down from the rear of the wagon. She was a buxom woman, not young but boldly handsome. She wore a gown with knee-length skirt. Beneath the edge of the gown, full Turkish pantaloons billowed coyly. Liz wore striped red and white silk stockings on her shapely legs, and high button shoes, with red tassels, that had been rather badly dented and scarred by rough travel on the trail.

Her two girls, Dot and Dolly, aroused by her shouts, crawled from the wagon, rubbing sleep from their eyes. They were young and shapely girls, dressed in duplicates of the gown and Turkish pantaloons favoured by Liz. As they followed after Liz and the teamsters, Jane Payne, escorted by Chicago Jack Hacker, overtook them.

"What's going on, girls?" Jane asked, in her breezy way.

CHAPTER X

"Find out for yourself, Miss Money Bags," Dot answered rudely, shrugging shoulders and tossing her black curls.

"Ask that shavetail who's been sparkin' you," suggested Dolly, puckering her mouth into a taunting smile, and patting her blonde hair.

Jane frowned and started to reply. But Chicago Jack, stepping past her, gave Dolly a rough push to thrust her aside.

"Stand aside for your betters," Chicago Jack rapped out.

Dolly drew her lips away from her teeth. She slapped at Jack's face with a clawing hand, and raked her nails down his smoothly shaven right cheek, leaving a bloody trail.

"You hellcat!" Chicago Jack snapped, and took the girl by the throat. He shook her until hairpins rained from her curls and all her long blonde hair tumbled down around her shoulders. She screamed and kept on pawing at his enraged face. Dot, doubling her hands into small fists, whirled and attempted to rush Jack. But big Red Dog, rumbling with laughter, stepped in and seized Dot in his arms.

Amazed at the fight that had so suddenly broken out between Chicago Jack and Sunset's biscuit shooters, Jane Payne jumped in and pulled Jack off the fighting, cursing Dolly.

"You should be ashamed of yourself!" she flamed. "Attacking a weak and innocent girl like Dolly."

"Come on, Miss Jane," growled Jack. "Let's get out of here. You don't sabe the West much."

And he hurried on toward the scene of the main fight, with Jane running at his heels.

"But why, Mr. Hacker," Jane asked, "did that girl talk about me and the lieutenant?"

"Because," Jack called back over his shoulder, "she's been tryin', ever since the train got stopped, to get that shavetail sweet on her. If you wasn't along, she figures she'd have him wrapped around her pink little finger in a jiffy."

"Oh," said Jane. "I see now."

They were approaching the dusty howling ring of men around Sam and the two corporals he had taken on. Just then the ring of men opened up and Jane saw Singin' Sam standing braced on his moccasins, choking Bootle, and slapping the fat corporal until he whined like a half-grown puppy.

"This," roared Sam, "is for hidin' out when them Sioux tried to jump that Payne gal!" And whack went Sam's hand on Bootle's bulging cheek. "This," Sam went on, using Bootle's other cheek, "is fer good measure! Runnin' the risk of lettin' a good-lookin', cornfed Missoury gal lose her pretty hair!"

"Oh," cried Jane, and put her hands to her flaming cheeks. *"Cornfed! Oh!"*

She saw one of the soldiers whip up his rifle and cover Sam. "Take your hands off Bootle!" the doughboy yelled. "You murderin' renygade! Take your hands off him!"

But before Sam could obey, Jane saw Chicago Jack Hacker whip a six-gun from his holster. Jack stepped in to where he covered Sam, with his pistol, from any attack by the soldiers.

"It's a fair fight," drawled Chicago Jack. "Don't none of you walkaheaps buy in."

Lieutenant Prime, breaking into the ring, checked the gunfight that threatened to flare between smiling Chicago Jack and the angry doughboys. Sharply, he ordered his men to return to their duty. "Keep your eyes peeled for Indians," snapped Prime. "We've already lost our ambulance and a good team of mules because you were all asleep on duty."

Sam speeded Bootle on his way with a swift kick in the pants. Spike Dillon was picking himself up from the earth, a bleeding wreck of a soldier. Prime swung angrily on the grinning mountaineer.

"What's the meaning of this?" he rapped out.

"Just what you see, Lieutenant," drawled Sam. "Had to whip two corp'rils."

"Don't you know you're under arrest for trespassing in Indian treaty territory?"

"I had sorta got the impression I was held fer murder, the way them doughboys turned me down. Men like that Dillon that I soldiered with—" And he nodded toward Spike, who was wiping blood off his battered face with a dirty neck scarf.

Prime nodded. "That's right," he answered. "I forgot! You're one of those infantry Slings, aren't you?"

Something in Prime's sharp voice made Sam bristle anew.

"And what's wrong with the infantry Slings?" he wanted to know, advancing on the stiff-backed young lieutenant.

But Prime wasn't a man who could be easily bluffed. He never gave way an inch to the angry Sam.

"Nothing wrong with them—*so far*," said Prime. Then he went on curtly, "If you don't stop this brawling with the soldiers of this train guard, I'll put you in irons."

Chicago Jack and the teamsters were watching and listening closely. A mutter ran through the dusty whiskered gang when the officer spoke of shackling Sam. But Prime turned sharply on them.

"Don't be fools," he said. "We have no time for brawling. We're three days from the river. There's plenty of Sioux watching us. Let's try fighting Injuns, not each other."

Sam, still bitter at the treatment he had received from the army, refused to be shamed by Prime.

"I thought," he jeered, "that it was now army policy to pet these danged war whoops instead of tryin' to kill 'em off like most of us want."

"You thought wrong," Prime said shortly.

"You and your soldiers are stoppin' American citizens from headin' north from the Platte to the Black Hills or to Montana. Ten years ago, the Bozeman Road was open and trains was halfway protected from war whoops by soldiers."

"You are familiar with the present situation, my man.

You know that this territory, between the Big Horns and the Black Hills, has been turned over to the Sioux by federal treaty. You know that you are not permitted to go north of the line of the Platte without official permission."

"Don't call me your man," Sam spat out. He stepped in closer to the officer. They were of similar height and weight. "I been my own man for the past four years since I took my discharge. I can shoot off my bazoo all I like to any corp'ril or green shave tail that hits this range—"

Sam had enjoyed his fight with Spike and Bootle so greatly that he had grown careless. Prime hadn't been long out of West Point, where cadets are trained to a fine point in the art of self-defence. Sam was grinning through his wiry whiskers as he talked to Prime. But he quit grinning and went down on his back when Prime snapped a quick jolting uppercut to his chin.

"You can shoot off your bazoo so long as you don't pick out the wrong man," said Prime, standing over Sam. "I owe you plenty for saving Miss Payne. But there are limits to what I'll take off a dirty skulker who apparently hated the army." He stepped away from Sam, and called in a sentry who was walking a post on the flank of the halted train.

"Stand guard on this man," he ordered, indicating Sam who was scrambling up with a black scowl on his face. "Keep him away from the mounted scouts! Find him a wagon to ride in. And you ride with him. But don't talk to him. You understand your orders?"

"Yes, sir," answered the brawny, moon-faced soldier.

"Your name is—" Prime inquired, frowning because he knew that he should have recalled this private's name without asking.

"Private Huffenberger, sir."

"Ah—How much service in, Private Huffenberger?"

"Six months, sir."

"A recruit, hey? Well, you don't know this prisoner at all. If he tries to talk to you, or any other soldier, cave in his head with the butt of your Springfield. You understand?"

"Yes, sir," Private Huffenberger said, and gave Prime the rifle salute when the lieutenant had stepped away from him.

Sunset Liz stepped up to Singin' Sam. She flashed him a smile and said in her sweetly husky way, "Sling—you can ride with me and the gals in my wagon."

Sam ran his eyes over the costume of Sunset Liz: the flaring skirt of scarlet, the puffed out pantaloons above red and white stockings, the tassels dangling from the high button shoes.

"Gosh," he gasped, "where did you hook onto such a rig, Sunset? Last time I see you in Cheyenne, you sported a velvet gown with a train that looked tuh be ten feet long. Enough gown, I declare, tuh build a wickiup for three Injuns."

"Go on with you, Sam Sling," laughed Liz, digging Sam in the ribs.

"You are sure togged out for the trail," he went on. "But ain't you apt to stampede your mules with them things you're sportin' so bold?"

Liz flung back her head and laughed loudly, showing her gold teeth all the way back. Then she hit Sam so heartily in the short ribs that he almost lost his wind. It was all in good fun.

"You are sure an ig'runt cuss," chortled Liz. "Didn't you ever hear tell of bloomers? Invented by a woman named Amelia Bloomer. She's so smart, and so hot on equal rights for women, that she aims to run fer president of these here United States."

"Hurray!" Sam cheered. "She gets my vote, you can bet your stack. And Shorty's too!"

"Where is that sawed-off little runt?" Liz asked. "Layin' out in the brush somewhere, drunk on Pete Narbo's trade whisky?"

Sam figured he talked enough with Liz. Thus far, he hadn't been questioned too closely about his sudden appearance when the Indians jumped the ambulance. He decided that Shorty and Tom had back-tracked off the peak the moment the train and the soldiers had driven off the Sioux. They'd be hiding out. Come dark, they'd make time hitting for the river with their horses and pelts. They would be cursing him out for getting himself taken by the army. They'd not thank him at all if he, by the least hint, indicated that they had been trespassing on Indian territory.

"Been a long time," he said cautiously, "since I seen Shorty drunk on Pete's brand of rotgut."

Liz assumed that he meant he hadn't been partnering with Shorty for some time. She forgot all about Shorty. She took him by the sleeve and started off toward her wagon. But Lieutenant Prime interfered. He told Liz, with a twisted smile on his face, that while Sam might know how to conduct himself in the wagon of Sunset Liz, he could not risk Private Huffenberger.

"Huffenberger is quite new to the West and its ways," Prime grinned, "so he'd better find a seat for the prisoner in a wagon occupied exclusively by the male sex."

Sunset Liz cocked an eye of roguish blue and measured the big fresh-faced recruit.

"Why, Lieutenant," she said virtuously, "how you do go on."

Liz tossed a kiss from the ends of her fingers to Sam, turned and ambled on past Jane Payne. She called back to Sam, "Take care of yourself, kid. We'll have a powwow when we get to the Platte."

Chicago Jack, holstering his gun, grinned at Sam. "That should be a real powwow," he drawled. He called to the teamsters, "One of you boys can find a seat in your wagon for Sam Sling."

"He can ride with me," bawled Red Dog. "Any hombre that can whip two corp'rils can ride free with me any old day."

Sam answered cheerfully enough, "Whipped two cor'prils, Red Dog! But this here shave tail walloped me." He winked at Prime. "When I wasn't lookin'."

Prime answered tartly, "After we get to the river, I'll be at your service any old time. Until then, as a prisoner, you'll obey orders or get Private Huffen—er—get that private's rifle stock in the head!"

When Sam was herded past Jane Payne by the strutting Private Huffenberger, he tried to halt and greet her. He was amazed at the blazing look in her blue eyes.

"Why, what's come over you, Miss Jane?" he inquired in a puzzled tone.

"Cornfed!" she flamed. "So you consider me *cornfed*?" *Whap!* Jane slapped his face.

"Hey!" barked the astounded Private Huffenberger, thrusting his rifle barrel and bayonet between the angry girl and the surprised mountaineer. "You can't attack my prisoner!"

"Take your old prisoner," Jane half-sobbed, "and give him back to the Injuns!" And she covered her eyes with her hands and fled from the scene.

Private Huffenberger thrust aside the teamsters.

"Stand away from the prisoner," he ordered, in his thick important voice. He then told Sam to step out toward Red Dog's wagon. "And walk in step," cautioned Private Huffenberger, falling in at Sam's heels. "You've been in the army. Step out in time. Hep, hep—"

Red Dog and his mates fell in behind Private Huffenberger in single file. They swung past the wagon from which Liz and her girls were watching and laughing.

"Hep, hep!" snapped Private Huffenberger, striding along with rifle at smart right shoulder arms.

"Hep, hep!" roared Red Dog, waving at Liz and the two girls. "Belly full of bean soup! Can't keep step!"

Half of a mind to turn around and bid Red Dog shut up, Sam glanced off to his outer flank. What he saw, out in the distant sagebrush vista made him forget his present troubles. On a distant ridge, he marked a man who had just dismounted from his pony. The man's blue uniform shone in the sunlight, informing Sam that he was a soldier. The man in blue was rapidly raising and lowering his rifle over his head. It was a familiar infantry signal to Sam Sling.

"Enemy in sight!" he yelled. "Turn out! Enemy in sight!"

CHAPTER XI

Sam's shout of alarm was echoed almost instantly by the crack of a Springfield rifle fired by one of the guards walking post afoot a few paces from the train.

"Turn out the guard!" the sentry bawled. "Turn out the guard. Enemy in sight!"

Private Huffenberger stood with gaping jaw gazing wide-eyed toward the distant picket who had sent the warning signal. The man had remounted and was galloping down through the sagebrush toward the train.

Red Dog and his fellow mule skinners, some cursing hostile Indians bitterly, scattered toward their teams and wagons. An army bugle began an insistent blaring of the assembly call from where the reserves of the train guard had eaten the noon meal.

Sam whirled around and, without another word of warning, raked the bayoneted rifle from the hands of Private Huffenberger. He snapped open the breech block, assured himself the gun held a shell in the chamber, then padded out to where blue-clad guards were bunching up in a thin skirmish line, all gazing toward the oncoming horseman.

On the distant ridge, so lately occupied by the galloper, a hand mirror began blinking flashes of light.

"Signals," Sam snapped as he came up to the line of guards. "Sioux talkin' across this valley."

The train had made its noon halt in a wide valley bounded by mountain foothills on the west and the ominous bare ridge to the eastward. On this latter ridge now appeared the enemy.

They would never be mistaken for white men. They were so far distant that even the colour of war ponies was dull.

But the free and easy way in which the men on the ridge rode back and forth, now bunching up, then fanning out into a skirmish line, indicated to all experienced plainsmen with the train that there rode the wild cavalry of the West, the warlike Sioux.

"Signals," growled the soldier who stood beside Sam. "What they sendin' signals for?"

So engrossed were the doughboys in watching the approach of their mounted scout that not one had glanced toward Sam as he ran up, trailing Private Huffenberger's rifle.

Nor had Sam taken time to look over the line of soldiers. All were alert, fearing that at any moment a knot of whooping red riders would dart from the brushy mouth of some hidden coulee, and cut down the gallant horseman who had signalled that the enemy was coming into sight.

But when the surly guard spoke up, Sam glanced at him and gasped, "Spike! Spike Dillon!"

Spike, as startled, turned his puffy face toward his late opponent.

"Sling!" he rapped out. "Sam Sling." Then, seeing the rifle in Sam's hands, he blinked his bloodshot eyes that were half hidden by folds of bruised flesh. "You're armed," he barked. "Where did you get a gun? Where—"

Sam started to explain that he had jerked it away from the hands of a startled recruit taken aback by his first adventure in standing off Indians. But he knew that serious charges would be preferred against Huffenberger if the army discovered that he had allowed a prisoner to disarm him.

So Sam told a little white lie to shield Huffenberger.

"We were up in the wagon when I saw the signal," he told Spike. "Huffenberger was getting settled. I grabbed the gun and jumped out before he saw what I was doing."

"Hand over that gun!" Spike ordered menacingly. "You're under arrest!"

Sam backed away from Spike, bringing the rifle to the ready, setting the hammer at full cock.

"Fergit that red tape," he said, between his teeth. "You

fool! There's probably Sioux in the hills on both sides of this train. That's why the signals are bein' flashed. They may jump us at any minute from both flanks. We'll need to bear down with every gun we got in this train.''

"You Injun-lovin' renygade," Spike spat out, "you only got one bullet in that piece.''

"I got a bay'nit on the barrel," growled Sam. "If I miss with the slug, I'll give you the long thrust through your gizzard!" His smoky grey eyes now carried a red look. His coarse black hair was blowing in the wind. As he talked to Spike, he kept on backing up, for Spike also carried a bayoneted rifle, and, to boot, carried a pistol on his cartridge belt. Sam wanted to get enough space between Spike and himself for the thrust and parry of bayonet fighting if Spike went through with his threat of disarming him.

After the first alarm, the wagons of the train had moved hurriedly but without confusion to shape up a corral for a barricade against Sioux slugs and arrows. Red Dog and his mates were all experieced in such manoeuvres, for they earned their bread driving their outfits through hostile Indian country. Each driver, once he had taken up his leather lines, shouted to his mules and followed the wagon just ahead. At a shout from Chicago Jack Hacker, apparently the captain of the train, the lead wagon turned and made a wide circle. When this had been completed, each wagon halted with its teams turned inwards. Drivers hurriedly freed nervous braying mules from the traces and herded them in the centre of the circle. Men were appointed to watch the stock. If war arrows flying over the tops of the wagons, wounded mules and threatened to stampede the stock, these guards would shoot down the injured animals to quiet the panic.

Where spaces intervened between the wagons, tongues were straightened out, and set up on single-trees to serve as obstacles against red horsemen who might attempt to ride through these spaces into the heart of the barricaded train.

Each wagon carried a huge wooden keg on its side for spare water. These would be opened and the water used if the

Indians attempted to fire the train by shooting flaming war arrows into the canvas covers.

All this manoeuvring took time but not as much as if the teamsters had been greenhorns. Every man worked without haste but made each move count.

Sam hadn't wasted a thought or a glance on the train. He felt satisfied that men like Chicago Jack and Red Dog would complete the barricade without difficulty. The present concern was to establish an outside line of skirmishers, ready to break any Indian charge with volleying Springfields if the Sioux launched an immediate rush.

But here was Spike Dillon, bitterly resentful because he had been mauled by Sam's fists, intent on his own narrow aim of disarming a prisoner, forgetful of the greater danger which now loomed.

"By Gawd," Sam swore at Spike, "if you don't get into line on the jump and be ready to shoot up the Sioux, I'll kill you if I hang for it at sunset. Are you rememberin', you fool, that we got some white women in this train?"

That touched Spike Dillon to the heart. Every plainsman and veteran soldier worried more about women than themselves in Indian fights.

Spike frowned, but he lowered the point of his bayonet. He stood glowering a moment at Sam. Then he growled, "Turn in that gun after the fight!"

"Sure," said Sam "What would I do with the blamed thing then?"

Spike nodded. He snapped a half-dozen cartridges from his web belt with practised fingers, handed them over to Sam. "We may need to fire more than one volley," he said: "You'll need spare ammunition."

Prime came jogging through, the dust on his boots. His face was flushed with excitement but he was steadying his line of men with a calm voice.

"Spread out," he ordered, trotting along the line. "Each of you take cover behind a rock or sagebrush. Don't fire a shot until you hear the bugle call of 'commence firing.'

B.S.—3*

After one volley, start dropping back to the wagons."

The lieutenant saw Sam hunting around for a buffalo wallow to hide in. He halted, with a frown on his face.

"You're a prisoner," he said. "But you're armed."

"Until things settle down," said Sam. "Then you can have your gun back."

Prime seemed to take Sam's promise at full value. He nodded and hurried on. The mounted scout now arrived at full tilt, pulling down his froth-mouthed pony sharply, lurching off his McClellan saddle with a salute to Prime. He turned and pointed to the distant ridge where the Sioux were scattering.

"Whole pack of them on the other side," he said hoarsely. "At least fifty, Lieutenant."

Prime nodded. "Glad you got in safely, Hobson. Take your horse inside the train. Then rejoin this skirmish line."

Sam, now flat on his belly, behind an ant hill, turned and gave Spike a grin.

"Fifty of 'em, he says. Supposin' there's fifty on the other flank. Ought to build up into a real scrap."

"We'll stop 'em," growled Spike. "A dozen soldiers and as many mule skinners, all armed with modern rifles against Sioux packin' bows and arrows, and some old smoothbore trade guns. It'll be like shootin' ducks."

"Yeah," Sam drawled. "I've been around ducks that was danged hard to shoot. You're forgettin', Spike, that you soldiers have single-shot guns and some of these warwhoops are beginnin' to pick up magazine rifles. Henrys and Winchesters. They pay high for 'em, I've heard. A pony load of beaver or buffalo for one gun or a box of fixed ammunition."

"You ought to know," Spike said, showing his teeth in a nasty grin. "We hear, at the cantonment, that you mountain men are makin' more money this year sellin' guns and shells to Injuns than tradin' with 'em for pelts, and usin' trade whisky and beads and such gimcracks to close your deals."

Sam answered hotly, "If we wasn't settled down to stop the Sioux, I'd black your eyes again for that, Spike. A lot of us mountain men got little use for a soldier, but we don't go so far as to help the Sioux butcher 'em."

"You and me," Spike rejoined as heatedly, "don't agree on a heck of a lot of things. When we get this train to the river—if we ever do—I'll try to beat out your brains, Sam Sling."

Sam took another long look at the Sioux warriors on the distant ridge. Now they were riding slowly down the slope, coming toward the train. He could hear the distant thud of pony hoofs against rocks, the hoarse chant of the warriors as they sang some sort of a war song. The sky was filled with big white fleecy summer clouds that occasionally passed over the sun. Suddenly the sunlight slanted down, boldly outlining the Sioux riders.

Sam counted a dozen warriors. Their paint and riding gear flashed and sparkled in the sunshine. They had taken particular care to paint up for this occasion. That puzzled Sam. They were not resorting to usual Sioux attack tactics. Riding down slowly that way. Singing their songs. Holding in their head-tossing ponies with taut buckskin war bridles.

The playful Wyoming wind tossed the dyed eagle feathers that fluttered from the lance heads carried by the Sioux. Louder grew the singing.

"Hagh!" the Sioux chanted. "Hagh! Hagh!"

"You sabe any of their danged lingo?" Spike asked.

"Some. They are singin' that this is a fine sunny day to kick you pony soldiers outa their buff'ler country."

"If it wasn't fer birds like you," Spike said bitterly, "we wouldn't be here."

"Is that what you boys all hold against me?" Sam asked curiously. "I figured I might get slung in the mill for jumpin' your fool line. But all you birds act like I had committed bloody murder, way you've been turnin' me down. Won't even tell me any news of the regiment or my brother."

"We got orders not to talk to you," Spike said shortly. "You'll find out soon enough what all the row's about when you get to the river."

Sam shook his head frowningly, vastly puzzled. So they had not forgotten to question him closely about his reasons for being so deep into Indian country. From the officer on down the line they were all under orders not to question too closely any prisoners they brought in. They were to deliver them at Cantonment Sparks where superior authority would do all the talking and questioning.

"There seems to be," Sam growled, "plenty of blood on the moon."

He wondered fleetingly if some word of the fight in the beaver meadow had reached the army. Surely they would not be charging his friends and himself with murder for killing a couple of Indians. The law hadn't become quite so well established on the frontier yet that fights between whites and Indians, in which men were killed, were regarded as material for solemn jury trials and ensuing hangmen's gallows.

No. The army simply rounded up trespassers north of the line and kicked them out. If red or white men were killed, the army regarded that as just so much hard luck for the dead men.

"Wagh!" sang the line of Sioux warriors, shaking their lances and rattling their medicine gourds in time to the weird chant. "Wagh! This is our buffalo land."

"I ought to sing 'em a song myself," growled Sam.

"Save it," snapped Spike.

Sam grinned. He lined out his spare cartridges to his front so that he could reach them easily. He wished he had been given time enough to find his Henry and hand gun. But the army had taken away his weapons. These old Long Tom Springfields would tear out a man's belly at two hundred yards. But you had to reload after every shot.

CHAPTER XII

Except for an occasional bray from a fretful mule, not a sound came from the barricaded train as the Sioux approached. Every rifleman was in his place, some under the wagons, others in the spaces between, protected by whatever gear they could pile up that would turn away arrows.

The line of soldiers, flat on their bellies behind rocks and brush and ant hills—these chosen because soft sand stopped a bullet about as easily as a rock and wasn't so apt to throw off cutting rock chips if hit by a glancing bullet—kept their narrowed eyes on the painted warriors.

The Sioux came on until they were not fifty yards from the skirmish line.

Soldier fingers itched to press triggers. But discipline restrained them. They had been ordered not to fire until they heard the bugle.

Sam licked his dry lips and whispered, half to himself, "They have let 'em come in too close."

Those swift little ponies could cross fifty yards before a man could draw two deep breaths. Half the skirmish line would fire, then reload hastily as their mates snapped a volley. But armed with single-shot guns, these soldiers were up against fearful odds against these swift and expert horsemen. Sam wondered why the army didn't equip its frontier troops with magazine rifles.

"More red tape," he snarled. "They got to lose a couple of regiments before they learn."

He was examining the Sioux closely. He was seeking some warrior with a blue army blouse buttoned around his sinewy brown body. He was also looking for his stolen buffalo horse, and for a chief who rode on a yellow pony. He didn't think he'd spot the stolen Indian woman with the war party. They seldom let squaws accompany fighting men. Even when it came to their horses, warriors on raids never used mares.

Then Sam saw something that put a spark of interest in his wary eyes.

"Hey," he called excitedly to Spike, "those war whoops are actin' like pony soldiers."

"What do you mean?"

"Dang it all, man. You a cor'pril and supposed to know the book. Can't you recognise a flag of truce?"

He heard Spike slowly expel his breath. "Gosh," whispered Spike, "you're right. A flag of truce. Maybe this won't be a fight today."

These doughboys would fight to the bitter end, but not a man there but knew that they were badly outnumbered by the Sioux. More of frontier army methods. Never enough soldiers on hand to handle the situation. Plenty of big talk by the generals but tough on the thin blue ranks forced to back up words with action.

A white rag did indeed flutter from the tip of a lance.

A single horseman carried it. He rode out in front of the line of Sioux warriors as the painted cavalcade came to a halt. Advancing for a half-dozen yards he halted, too. He waved the lance suggestively. The white flag fluttered in the gentle wind.

The horsemen had come so near that Sam's sharp eyes recognised his squat body, slouched in a Mexican-style saddle, and the thick black beard that half masked his face. Sam cursed and spat into the ant hill, drowning a half-dozen big black ants.

"You know him?" Spike asked.

"Sure do. That's Narbo. Canady Pete Narbo. I bought my winter grubstake from him last fall."

"What's he doin' with these Injuns? Is he a 'breed?"

"Don't know for sure. He comes from the north. Been tradin' with the tribes for years. Talks a half-dozen lingos. Army uses him a lot as interpreter."

Canada Pete kept on vigorously waving his flag of truce.

The Sioux had ended their war song. They were holding in their ponies, closely watching the train and its guards.

Prime stepped out in front of the skirmish line.

"Careful, Lieutenant," Spike called out.

Prime nodded. But he stood stiff as a poker, facing the Indians and Canada Pete.

"You're all covered," he called to Canada Pete. "I'll open fire if your Indians come a step nearer this train."

"They ain't my Injuns," Pete complained. "They brought me up from my tradin' post to talk to you. Killed a pony gettin' me here. Let me come in closer where I won't strain my voice."

"Come in alone," said Prime. "But tell them to stay where they are."

Pete turned and talked earnestly to the halted warriors. They nodded. He spurred his pony. He came in slowly until he had reached the waiting officer and the line of hard-eyed soldiers. The trader was a bulky man in his dirty buckskins and thick hair and beard. He wore an old slouch hat and knee-high moccasins on his legs.

"He hasn't got a rifle on his saddle," Sam whispered to Spike. "He may be tellin' the truth about the Injuns fetchin' him up here for a powwow."

"I don't trust nary white who's so danged intimate with war whoops," growled Spike. "If they try anythink funny, I'll put my first bullet through the bright right eye of Canady Pete."

"I'll take that buck just behind him," said Sam, "who's all painted up fancy as a Pennsylvany Dutch farmer's barn in streaks of red and white."

Canada Pete, knowing that he had aroused the suspicion of the troopers, leaned from his saddle and talked in an aggrieved whine to Prime.

"I can't help bein' here," he said. "You know me, Lieutenant. I've done lots of things for the army. Capt'in Budhouse trusts me. I hold a trader's permit from the army. It's like I say. A couple of these Sioux bucks routed me out at first dark last night. I'm rode down to a whisper. But they told me they wanted you to get word from their chief from a white man you could trust."

"Who is this chief?"

"He is called the Kicking Horse. He stands high in the Sioux nation."

"Where is he?"

"I don't know. Probably back in those hills where they got a pretty big camp."

"I'd prefer to see this Kicking Horse, eye to eye. He's already broken the treaty by attacking us."

"He aims," drawled Canada Pete, "to attack you some more, Lieutenant."

"We're ready for him."

"But he wants me to tell you he won't waste warriors and ponies burnin' this train. He's callin' for help. He aims to make his big attack on Cantonment Sparks. He says he can bring a thousand warriors down to take the hair of all the pony soldiers."

"I think a battalion of infantry will prove that his aim was bad," Prime said dryly.

"Think what you like, Lieutenant. I'm just deliverin' the message of the Kicking Horse. He says the army has broken the treaty by letting white men go into the Big Horns and take Sioux beavers. He says when the Injuns tried to capture these trespassers, your troops protected 'em. That Sioux were killed by soldiers while trying to run these trespassers out."

"The treaty states that the army shall handle all white trespassers. The chief knows that."

"The Kicking Horse wants me to tell you," Pete persisted, "that right now you are holding one of these trespassers. There were three of them, but two got away. He figures he can catch two of them. He says that if you'll turn over the man you caught, then he'll call off the attack on Cantonment Sparks."

Sam tensed. So he was the centre of this whole deal. The army, which didn't like him very much, could turn him over

to the Kicking Horse and halt the outbreak of another large
Sioux war. Sam knew well enough what would happen to
him if he were delivered to the Kicking Horse. Rawhide
Buttes got the name from a delivery of that sort in the early
days. Indians could skin a man alive and take hours to do it.
The inside of Sam's mouth felt dry and rough as cotton. For
a long time he hadn't worried much about the arrow wound
in his side, but now he began to feel it anew. In fact, lying
here under the hot sun, he could feel every inch of his lanky
body. Never had that body seemed so dear to him as this
minute. Never had the sun felt so warm. Never had life
seemed so sweet as it did now when Sam Sling lay on his
hollow, retching stomach and looked past Canada Pete into
the impassive painted faces of Sioux horsemen.

Then Prime spoke, and shortly. "Go back and tell your
chief—"

"Not my chief, Lieutenant."

"Go back and tell this Kicking Horse that the army does
not take prisoners just for the fun of turning them over to the
Sioux. Tell the Kicking Horse to go out and catch his own
prisoners."

"If I go back and talk like that, Lieutenant," Pete whined,
"he'll likely scalp me."

A new hot voice broke into the powwow. Chicago Jack
Hacker loomed up suddenly at the side of Prime. Hacker's
right hand was hard on his holstered gun. He glared up at
Canada Pete. And the interpreter, startled, sat up straight in
his saddle.

"You double-crosser," snarled Chicago Jack. "You Injun-
lovin' double-crosser! By the livin', I ought to shoot you off
your pony."

Canada Pete stared down at the angry plainsman with a
bewildered look on his bearded face.

"Now, Jack," he whined complainingly, "that shore ain't
no way to say How to an old friend. You musta been
drinkin' heavy."

"None of *your* mountain lion sweat," sneered Jack. "You

know what I mean. It stands. I see now why the danged army stopped this train. You tipped 'em off. You was the only man knew which way I figured to head." He swung on the lieutenant. "I reckon that's why you overtook us."

Prime answered brusquely, "No time now to talk about that. Get back to your wagons. Our important business, right now, is this powwow with the Sioux."

Chicago Jack shrugged, said harshly to Pete that they'd meet again, then stalked angrily back to the train. He passed Sam Sling, who was also watching Pete and thinking deeply. Sam was recalling that Pete had outfitted his partners and himself the autumn before they made ready for the Big Horn trip. The suspicion took firm root in Sam's mind that Pete had plotted and perhaps taken part in the recent raid which had led to the murder of Buffalo Hump and the loss of the Night Star. Sam determined that when the time was ripe he too, would see Pete again.

"Go back to the Kicking Horse," Prime said to Canada Pete. "Tell him if he tries anything like raiding this train or the cantonment, the Washingtons will send heap big bunch of walkaheaps and pony soldiers, even wagon guns, to fix him."

"I'd shore hate to see you give these reds a white man," Pete said soothingly. But he shook his shaggy head, gazing toward the train. "You're shore runnin' powerful chances of losin' your women to the Sioux."

"They must run their chances. They came up here as trespassers."

"The Kicking Horse will be mad," said Pete, turning his pony.

Sam Sling slouched out, trailing the Springfield.

"Wait a minute," he drawled amiably.

CHAPTER XIII

At the sight of Sam, the Sioux to the rear of Canada Pete began chattering like a flock of enraged magpies. Sam grinned broadly and began to taunt them in their own lingo. He asked them what had happend to their strong war medicine? It seemed that one lone long hair could still whip a dozen of their best men. Perhaps they had better get back to camp and send the boys out to fight while they did work for the squaws.

Canada Pete rolled his eyes. "So you're the hombre they want," he said, as though vastly surprised. "So I reckon the two that got away must be your pards, Rocky Mountain Shorty and Tom Bear Mouth, that Shoshone."

"Are you so danged surprised, Pete? And what's the latest St. Louis auction price on prime winter beaver fresh out'n the Big Horns?"

Pete licked his thick lips. "I don't know what you're drivin' at," he answered sullenly.

"Chicago Jack claims you tipped off the army to his train headin' north. I'm beginnin' to think you tipped off the Sioux to our camp in the Big Horns. You was the only white man who knew enough about our plans, last fall, to trail us into the mountains. You could let us get in a winter's trappin', spy on us, and when the time was right, get a big drag of beaver pelts."

"Now that's a danged lie," Pete said hotly. "If I wasn't tied up here on this powwow business, I'd get off and fight you for such talk."

"If the army wasn't keepin' cases on me, Pete, I'd haul you off your war pony and make you fight."

Prime broke in angrily. "You two are holdin' up this train arguing like this."

Sam nodded, still amiable. "That's right, Lieutenant. I just wanted to point out that I figure this Pete is a renegade.

He's sellin' out his own blood to hostile Indians. I'd bet a bale of prime beaver that he hasn't been near the Platte River for the past four or five days. He's been up in the Big Horns, figurin' how to murder a good man so he can steal his wife."

With a snarling curse, Canada Pete came off his horse, snaking a bowie knife from his beaded belt as his moccasin toes hit the hardpan. He ducked his head and ran in on Sam, knife point thrown forward in the hope of ripping open Sam's lean belly. The army had taken away Sam's skinning knife, but he was carrying a long rifle with a bayonet fixed to the barrel. He pitched the rifle forward as Pete came in, and drove the bayonet through the slack of Pete's right sleeve. The furious trader struggled to free himself, mouthing out curses that no man could call him a renegade and live to boast about it. Sam held him off, laughing as he watched Pete's struggles.

At Prime's shout, soldiers rushed up and seized both men. The Sioux escort had become excited. They were crowding their nervous ponies nearer the train.

Prime roared, "First squad! Make ready! Prepare to fire!

Up went the rifles of eight doughboys, sights covering the Sioux. The Indians heard the snick of gun hammers being cocked, looked into the black muzzles of walkaheap guns that could kill at a mile. Sullenly they backed their ponies.

"Cor'pril," Prime said to Spike Dillon, "keep those Sioux covered. Open fire with your squad if they start anything."

"Now," Prime turned on Pete, "mount up and get back to your chief with my message."

Pete rubbed his arm sullenly, his dark gaze intent on grinning Sam Sling.

"I'm not forgettin' this," he threatened.

"Nor me," Sam assured him.

Pete thrust a moccasin toe into his wooden stirrup and mounted up. Sam noted that he went into the saddle, Indian style, on the right side of his pony.

A soldier returned the bowie knife to the trader. Pete, with a last glare at Sam, began turning his pony.

"Wait a minute," said Sam. He turned to Prime. "Let's make this a real sportin' event," he said. "That Kickin' Horse seems to want me bad. And looks like the army figures I got 'em into this mess with a whole caboodle of female folks. Now here's my proposition, Lieutenant. Loan me a fast pony. Give me my Henry rifle, shell belt, hand gun and knife—and a hundred yards start on those war whoops. And the Kickin' Horse can call off any attack on this train or Cantonment Sparks."

Canada Pete looked down and sneered, "White brave."

"Ask your pet Injuns," Sam persisted. Then he flung back his head and began to sing:

"Oh take me back to the buff'ler days,
When Injuns whooped in the prairie haze,
But when the Sioux met a lone white man,
They turned their rumps and ran and ran."

He broke off his weird chant with more comments on Sioux styles of fighting. He was striking deeply at their fierce pride and their superstitious belief in their war medicine. He wound up by asking them what had become of the pony soldier's coat. And why didn't they play war music on the pony soldier's bugle horn? Was it still true that the Sioux of the Kicking Horse band had been sired by skunks and jack rabbits? If they were real men, and their medicine was strong, surely they'd gamble on being able to run down one lone white.

The Sioux would have ridden straight down on Sam if the army rifles had not held them back. They set up a wolfish yelping. And finally Canada Pete said, with a shrug, to Prime, "They say it's a bet. Turn loose this wolf. And there'll be no fight on your train or the cantonment."

Sam laughed and said to the iron-faced lieutenant, "I'll go back and pick out a pony."

But Prime answered sharply, "You'll stand right here. The army does not require this show of heroism on your part." He turned to Pete. "This man is our prisoner. Tell the Kicking Horse to come to the cantonment peacefully and the pony soldier chief will smoke a pipe and talk with him about this fight in the Big Horns. If this man who sings has shown a bad heart, the army will punish him by putting him in the big stone corral."

Pete jeered at Sam. "You and your fool singin'." He nodded to the officer. "I'll tell the chief," he went on, "but I don't think it'll make his heart good. You better get set for plenty of trouble, Lieutenant."

Pete rode slowly to his waiting braves. Sam watched him depart, a black frown on his face. He turned angrily on Prime. "I meant what I said. I wasn't trying to show off."

"Nobody accused you of that. You're our prisoner. It's our order to return you and these other trespassers to Cantonment Sparks for questioning by the commanding officer." He turned to Spike Dillon as Pete and the Sioux rode slowly away through the sagebrush. "Deploy as skirmishers until the train is hooked up. Then take your usual posts as advance, rear, and flank guards. I'll be with the advance wagon."

"Yes, sir," said Dillon. He nodded toward Sam. "What about the prisoner?"

"Disarm him and turn him over to Private Huffenberger." Prime frowned and looked around him. "Where is Huffenberger?"

Huffenberger stalked up. He was carrying a gun. It was Sam's pet Henry rifle. He snapped his heels together and gave Prime the rifle salute. The lieutenant noted that the private was not armed with the proper style of weapon. Sam cut in angrily before Prime could explode over the head of the luckless soldier.

"I grabbed his rifle away while we were climbing into Red Dog's wagon," he said. "The rookie couldn't help it. I was pretty scairt," Sam curled his lip, "at the way you had told him to cave in my ornery head. I was tryin' to get plumb away."

"Take him back," Prime said to Huffenberger. "This time see that he doesn't get away with your piece. Follow my former order. Cave in his head with the butt if he makes another funny move."

"Yes, sir," said Huffenberger. He took back the rifle which Sam had jerked from his grip at the first sign of Indians. A grinning soldier passed it over. But now Huffenberger found himself vastly puzzled. He was carrying two rifles. Army regulations did not prescribe the manner in which a guard should carry two rifles.

"What are you waiting for?" barked Prime. He had turned away and was ordering the teamsters to hook up and string out.

"Which goes on the right shoulder?" stammered Huffenberger.

Prime shook his head, then held out a hand. "Oh, give me that Henry," he said, in a weary tone.

Huffenberger, thankfully relieving himself of the Henry, fell Sam smartly into line, executed an about face, and marched him off to the train. As Sam approached the wagons, he saw the grinning whiskery face of Red Dog and heard the muleskinner's song.

> "Hep! Hep! Belly full of bean soup!
> Can't keep step!

The mules were hooked up with many loud yells of "Gee" and "Haw." Sam sat in the high seat of Red Dog's wagon, baffled and angry. This train might be attacked and taken by the Kicking Horse before it reached the river. Sam felt that somehow, as a trespasser into Indian territory, he had aroused the anger of the Sioux. He had figured, when he offered to outrun the Sioux, that he stood a fifty fifty chance or saving his hair. He had been certain of one thing, and that was that if they overtook him, he would not be taken alive for their torture fire.

As the wagons lined up for the roll-out, he could hear the chatter of Sunset Liz and her girls coming from the covered wagon that followed Red Dog's.

Red Dog climbed up and kicked off the brakes. From the head of the train came a high-pitched yell of "Roll Out!"

Mule skinners cracked their whips, began talking loud blue mule language. Red Dog gathered up his ribbons and picked a fly off the long ear of his balky leader with his silk whip popper. Wheels began slowly to revolve as the mules put their shoulders against their collars. The train was under way, heading for Cantonment Sparks.

But now the soldiers of the train guard were vigilant. They lined both flanks, eyes ever turned toward the hills where the Sioux undoubtedly were waiting and watching. Three well-horsed scouts rode in the advance. A strong rear guard was commanded by Corporal Spike Dillon. Chicago Jack galloped back and forth along the train, aiding teamsters who had trouble getting over high centres, keeping a weather eye out for Indians. Jack reined in once by Red Dog's wagon when the whole train had checked for a breather before starting up a steep grade.

CHAPTER XIV

By order of Lieutenant Prime, the wagon train made an early evening halt, formed its corral, and unhooked the mule teams. Under strong guard, the work stock was herded near the camp for grazing on the bunch grass. Fires were lit, the evening meal put on to cook. But Prime passed out the word that when darkness came on, the train would commence a night march. Campfires would be built and left burning to deceive any Indian scouts who might be watching from surrounding hills.

Sam ate his supper with Red Dog and two other team-

sters. Private Huffenberger also received civilian rations
which he took gratefully, since they were of better quality
than the march meals being served to his fellow soldiers.
Chicago Jack dropped down by the fire for a bit of talk as
the sun began sinking back of the western hills.

Sam enjoyed his supper of mulligan stew based on dried
buffalo meat, strong unsweetened black coffee, and baking
powder bread cooked in a frying pan. Meanwhile Huffenberger bent so eagerly over the appetising mulligan that Sam
got in a few words of private talk with Chicago Jack.

Since joining the train, Sam had been curious as to why
the train had gone far north into Indian territory while Jane
Payne believed her wagons were being guided west to the
Sweetwater mining region which was open to pale face settle-
ment and trade. Jack laughed about that when Sam made
inquiry.

"Jane and her guardeen, that old jasper with the grey whiskers you see around here, they're greenhorns," Chicago Jack
explained, laughing. "They brought out a big stock of
groceries by rail to Cheyenne, then freighted up to Cantonment Sparks. Seems like the girl is an orphan and sunk all her
inherited stake in the stuff. She went strong on flour, as she
had heard big talk of high prices for same in the minin' country. Like hundred dollars a hundred weight for flour, even
twenty-eight dollars for a small sack. Course she's got her
sights set too high for Sweetwater, where they can freight
stuff in from the railroad durin' summer season."

"Flour and such would bring high prices in Montana," said
Sam, "with the Bozeman Road closed."

"Yeah. I sorta pointed that out to the girl's guardeen, ol'
Barberry. The old fellow was willin' to take a chance on
Injuns if I'd guide the train north. So he kinda explained to
Jane that we had to make a big swing north to find better
grass along the trail for our mules."

"And in so doin'," Sam said coldly, "you got turned back
by the army and danged near massacred by the Sioux. If the
girl had lost her hair, Jack, you and her guardeen would be

all to blame. That ought to be somethin' for you to laugh about now that this Kickin' Horse is ready to jump us any time he feels able."

"Now don't get sore-headed at me, Sam," Jack objected. "This ain't the first train that ever got north without bein' checked by soldiers or Injuns. Only reason you're puttin' up the big talk," he grinned, "is because—like most all us men —you been makin' eyes at Miss Jane Payne."

Sam choked on his coffee. He set his tin cup on the earth and got up, ready to fight. But a hoot of laughter from Jack and the teamsters shamed away his wrath. They were all sweet on the greenhorn Missouri girl. They admitted it cheerfully.

"Liz has throwed in with me," Jack said, speaking low so that Huffenberger wouldn't hear him. "I can tell you she ain't packin' much flour in them barrels in her wagon. Course they are writ out as flour on the bill of ladin' she showed to the army at Cantonment Sparks. En route to South Pass in open territory." Jack winked. "That's why she has to wait until dark to refill her jug with pain killer. Two of them barrels is nigh brimful of pain killer that'll sell high in Montany."

"So Liz knew she was headin' for Montana?"

"Shore. She's an old-timer. Take a big chance for that Montany gold money. Same with Dot and Dollie. Why, them Montany miners'll pay a dollar a dance up there in any hurdy gurdy dance house."

So Jane Payne was the only innocent lawbreaker in the train. Even her guardian had winked at the breach of army regulations in the hope of making a big gain in Montana.

Sam's anger was stirred at thought of the risk to which the girl and her property had been put, but he could not raise any loud objections to the plans of Jack and old Barberry. He had been engaged in similar lawless activities all winter. He could, of course, warn Jane Payne if the train reached the river safely, that she must separate her wagons from Jack's guidance. There would not be much point now in explaining what a great risk she had taken unwittingly.

"You called Candy Pete today, hard," Sam said. "Told him he had double-crossed you."

"He did," Jack answered. Then he added cautiously, with a glance around the campfire circle and a lowering of his voice, "He tipped off the army about this train headin' north. That's why we got stopped. It was all Pete's fault in the first place."

"How come?"

"He was supposed to have stuff on the train, headin' for Montany. He got tied up on some other trade. Was away from his post when we pulled out. He thought I had turned him down." Jack raised his cup and spoke in a whisper as he held the cup to his lips. "But while I was ridin' outside circle this afternoon, I found the shoulder bone of a buffalo. Pete had left it for me. You know how messages are writ out here on the trail on buff'ler bones. He had writ fer me to meet him about first dark around the mule herd. Got a new deal to talk over."

Sam tensed. But he kept his voice calm as he asked Jack, "How'll you find him?"

"We've dealt before. He'll signal where he is. Three owl hoots. Keep it up until I locate him. Them soldiers on guard will never suspicion anything from the hootin' of an owl. That's why Injuns and hombres like us use owl talk for signalin'."

Red Dog broke up the talk with a loud demand that Sam sing a verse from his buffalo song. Sam didn't feel like singing tonight. He had determined that he would overhear the pow-wow between Jack and Canada Pete if he could outwit his guard.

He could look down the line of fires and see the women of the train eating their suppers. Jane was laughing merrily as she sat on a blanket at the side of Lieutenant Prime, plying knife and fork on a tin plate.

Now and then Prime joined in with his pleasant baritone laughter. It irritated Sam. He had saved her hair from the Sioux, but now she wouldn't throw him a pleasant word or a

smile. Seemed she had taken offence because he had called her a
cornfed from Missouri. He had meant it as a compliment.

"Well, here she goes, boys," Sam drawled, and throwing
back his shaggy head, he cocked his eye at the first star to
twinkle in the evening sky.

> "Oh—take me back to the buff'ler days,
> When Injuns whooped in the prairie haze,
> Deadwood gals show you a high old time,
> But Missoury cornfeds wasn't wuth a dime."

That verse checked the mingled laughter of Jane and
Lieutenant Prime. But it brought the corporal of the guard on
the angry gallop to Red Dog's fire. The corporal tonight was
Spike Dillon. He was riding a tough brown Indian pony, and
carrying his Springfield across his saddle fork.

"Pipe down on that fool singin'," he told Sam angrily.
"You want to bring the Injuns down on us?"

"Nothin' wrong with my singin'," Sam answered sullenly.
"Red Dog and these other hombres don't object. Of course,"
he raised his voice so that it would carry to Jane's fire, "some
other greenhorns might be too danged nice to like it."

"Special orders for the night, now goin' into effect, is for
you to shut up," Spike rapped out. He nodded to Huffenberger, who had jumped up and come to attention. "See that
he keeps his bazoo shut from now on."

"Yes sir," answered Huffenberger.

"Don't call me sir," snapped Spike. "You only say that
to an officer."

Sam stood up, grinning. "A corporal in the infantry," he
drawled to Huffenberger, "is about the lowest form of life
there is. Don't waste no politeness on him at all."

"You shut up, Sling" Spike snapped. "Little more chin
music from you and we'll gag and hog-tie you."

Chicago Jack, Red Dog, and the other teamsters were listening with wide grins, to the angry confab between Sam and
Spike. They were also enjoying the discomfiture of Huffen-

berger, still at strict attention, and vastly puzzled as to just how to address Dillon with respect.

"You might call him sweetheart," Red Dog suggested.

"Or darling," said another.

"What's a dog robber?" asked Jack. "Ain't that some kind of a corp'ril?"

But Dillon glared down at them with cold anger. "Don't forget you're all prisoners. The army is issuin' orders tonight in the hopes of savin' this train from the Sioux. What we're up against is not a laughin' matter. If there's any gent or gents want to buck the army further"—he ran his eyes over the circle of bearded men around the fire—"we can show 'em *quick* how wrong they are."

Chicago Jack stood up and stretched his arms. "Aw, Corp'ril," he drawled, "we didn't mean anything. Just a little joshin' to make us forget the danged war whoops." He glanced up at the darkening sky. "We'll be hookin' up in another hour," he went on. "I reckon I'll get in a little sleep until then."

But as he strolled off, Sam knew that Jack wished to get away from the corporal so that the latter could not interfere with his intended meeting with Canada Pete out by the grazing mule herd.

Sam was putting his own mind to ways and means of listening in on that powwow. Spike Dillon would be a difficult man to outwit tonight. But poor old Huffenberger, although he always meant well, was a big green recruit. So Sam dragged a blanket from the wagon and announced that he would roll up under the vehicle for a little sleep.

"He's tricky," Dillon cautioned Huffenberger. "Keep your eyes peeled."

"Shucks," Sam complained, crawling under the wagon, "where would I escape tonight? With that Kickin' Horse and his war whoops prowlin' the ridges."

"You're one man," Spike answered tartly, "we don't take any chances on."

Sam rolled up in the coarse blanket so that not even his

toes or the tip of his black head was in sight. Red Dog, glancing under the wagon as he fed sagebrush to the flickering fire told Sam he would sweat himself to death like a sick Indian in a medicine wickiup. But Sam only grunted, and humped up under the blanket like a couple of sacks of flour.

The supper fires had been built outside the wagon corral so that men could keep an eye on the chain guard of soldiers, and the herd of grazing mules. There was always the fear that the Indians might attempt to stampede the herd.

Huffenberger sat down with his back to one of the huge rear wheels of the wagon where he could keep an eye on Sam beneath the vehicle and listen to the teamsters talking around their fire.

Dusk began to fall swiftly, for the sun had long since disappeared. A chill little breeze began to blow from the north.

"That Sam Sling wasn't so locoed when he rolled up that way," said Red Dog. "I reckon I'll get out my buff'ler coat."

The fireside circle broke up, teamsters strolling off toward their wagons for a short rest before the mules were brought in for the night march. Sam heard the small noises of the camp die away. Shadows were deepening across the range. Spike Dillon rode past on another round of his guards, and Huffenberger sprang to his brogans with a clatter of belt and rifle.

Sam seized that moment to work his way out from under the blanket. He humped it up as though his body still reposed under its folds. He lay in the black shadow cast by the rear wheel opposite Huffenberger. Listening intently, he heard Spike caution the guard anew, and Huffenberger's reply that the prisoner was fast asleep. When the corporal had ridden on around the train, Huffenberger resumed his seat with back to the wheel near the fire, and feet stretched out to get its warmth on his toes.

Sam felt a pang of remorse at his escape, which might put poor Huffenberger in the guard-house when the train reached the river. But as he squirmed away from the wagon, circling his way down the inside line of the train, he told himself that he would return if he succeeded in overhearing the talk between

Jack and Pete. He felt almost convinced that it was Pete who had betrayed the trappers to the Sioux.

The crawling mountain man encountered only one moment of danger before he slid under a wagon, down the line, and snaked his way toward the mule herd. He ran almost head on into Sunset Liz as she emerged from the rear of her wagon. She was carrying a bottle. Although Sam was moving on silent moccasins, she sensed his approach, and turned with an exclamation of alarm.

"Hist," he whispered harshly, "it's only me. Sam Sling."

She confronted him, tightly gripping the black bottle.

"What are you after?" she asked. "A drink of pain killer?"

"It ain't dark yet."

"I'll wait then. Don't let the danged army know you seen me." And he slipped off into the shadows.

Out in the tall sagebrush that grew between the train and the mule herd, he lay flat on his stomach, listening for the measured hoot of an owl. The first darkness had covered the earth. Behind him, the line of fires had been built up brightly in response to Prime's order. Then came the signal intended to guide Chicago Jack to the meeting with Canada Pete.

Sam followed the direction of the call. He grinned in the darkness, edging his silent way past a sentry whose thudding boots could be heard for a hundred yards. If Indians were not fearful of the darkness, he thought, they could slip easily past any soldier guard, however vigilant.

He lay waiting, and the owl hoot reached his ears for the second time. Pete was growing impatient, waiting for Jack. If Jack didn't hurry, the mules would be brought in, and hooked up for the night march.

The third call from Canada Pete led Sam to the rim of a little shallow draw where the trader awaited Chicago Jack.

CHAPTER XV

Sam's first impulse was to take Pete by the throat and force from him a confession. Since his arrest by the army as a trespasser, it had lain heavily upon Sam's mind that in saving Jane Payne from the Sioux he had unwillingly betrayed the driving interest in life of his two partners. Tom Bear Mouth and Shorty had vowed not to rest until they had avenged the murdered Buffalo Hump and his missing wife, the Night Star.

But Canada Pete was not a sentry with untrained ears like Private Huffenberger. Pete would not be taken easily. At the first alarm, he'd slip away in the darkness toward the pony which he had undoubtedly hidden outside the camp before arranging this meeting with Chicago Jack.

Sam restrained his burning desire to achieve something that might square his account with Bear Mouth and Shorty. He lay in the shadows above the coulee, silent as a dead man, until he heard a rustle of movement in the brush, the low challenge from Canada Pete, and the answer of Chicago Jack in a harsh whisper.

Sam cursed himself for not attempting to crawl nearer the two frontiersmen. But he dared not run the risk. He lay there, straining his ears but hearing nothing except a low rumble of talk. Chicago Jack spoke out once in an angry, argumentative tone, but Pete cooled him off with his usual line of soothing whining talk.

Just what deal the two had struck, Sam could not ascertain. He heard only one sentence from Pete that changed his plan for the night. Just before Jack began his stealthy retreat to the train, Pete said rather sharply. "I can't tell for sure until I get to Paint Rock Sinks. The chief's there."

"You're double-crossin' again."

"No. You're safe until I can go and come from Paint Rock."

Chicago Jack growled. "I guess I got to trust you."

In the darkness, the two parted. Sam lay deep in thought. He could find his way, even by night, to Paint Rock Sinks. it was far off the beaten trail in an eroded desert country that lay around twenty miles north of the river. It had gained its name from deposits of coloured minerals in the rocks from which Indians manufactured their paint.

There would be a moon tonight, but Sam didn't intend to attempt the trailing of Canada Pete.

Capturing the range-wise trader by night would be more difficult than shooting fish. But if he could secure a mount, Sam thought he might scout out Paint Rock Sinks before dawn came. If the Kicking Horse had established his main camp there, such a venture appeared so dangerous that Sam dared not consider the risks involved. But he felt that he owed it to Tom and Shorty to risk his life in the attempt. He might see or hear something that would lead to revenge for Buffalo Hump and the Night Star. There was also the forlorn chance that he might gain some knowledge that would benefit the wagon train.

Huffenberger, of course, would wind up in the guard-house. But Sam told himself, rather uneasily, the army wouldn't bear down too hard on a raw recruit for allowing a prisoner to escape. Of course Spike Dillon, corporal of the guard, would also come in for punishment. But Sam shrugged off the thought of Spike. Let Spike lose his chevrons. He'd learn not to turn on an old-time bunky so harshly.

Sam was working his way out to the grazing mule herd in the hope of gaining a mount somehow. Of course, he'd be forced to make a bareback ride. His waist belt, and the trailing lariat of the mule he caught, must suffice as a crude sort of bridle. He wasn't certain as to just what the mule would do once he attempted to capture and ride the beast. The entire guard might turn out shooting.

Luckless Spike Dillon, making another round of the guards before the herd was driven in, solved the problem for Sam.

The corporal rode past Sam, who was hiding behind a

B.S.—4

sagebrush. Fifty yards ahead, a sentry challenged sharply,
"Who's there?"

Spike sang out, "Corporal of the guard!"

The sentry had heard the thud of hoofs. Complying with
strict army regulations, he issued his order.

"Dismount! Advance to be recognised."

Infantry guards never permitted a horseman to ride down
upon them.

Spike checked his pony. He slid from the saddle, tied a rein
to the top of a nearby bush and began walking slowly toward
the waiting sentry.

Here was Sam's chance to gain a mount, all saddled and
bridled. Furthermore, at the expense of Spike Dillon. He had
but to wait until Spike had reached the sentry. In the poor
light, then, if Spike sighted him mounting up he'd be too far
off to recognise Sam. But Sam's impulsive nature overcame
the caution which Tom Bear Mouth and Shorty had attempted
to instil into him. He wanted to get away from the army,
head south, scout out the camp of the Kicking Horse in Paint
Rock Sinks. He could not wait for Spike to reach the sentry.
He slid silently out from his covering sagebrush and
approached Spike's pony.

As he untied the bridle rein, the Indian pony flung back
its head with a snort of alarm.

Ten yards away, Spike Dillon whirled, flinging up his
Springfield.

Sam was jerking the pony around to protect himself from
Spike's bullet as he got into the saddle. The pony was stubborn: a hard-headed, iron-mouthed brute. Sam gasped out
an angry curse. "Stand hitched, you danged keghead!"

"Sling!" Spike Dillon roared, cocking his rifle. "Sling!
You're under arrest!"

Sam got a toe in swinging stirrup. The pony was uneasy
because he was mounting from the left or white man's side.
He had forgotten, in his hurry, that this was an Indian digger,
and that Indians always mounted from the right side.

Dillon wouldn't fire without another challenge. He was

lunging toward Sam as the latter struggled into the McClellan saddle.

"Sling!" Spike cried again. "Is that you, Sling? Get off my horse!"

Spike wasn't certain as yet that it was Sam. He had gone at first only by the sound of Sam's voice as Sam cussed the pony.

Now Sam had gained the saddle. He kicked the pony in the ribs.

The sentry, awaiting his corporal, heard the drumming of hoofs as the pony broke into a gallop. He was puzzled at the sound, but true to orders, he roared out an alarm, firing a shot from his rifle.

"Turn out the guard!" he bellowed. "Post Number Three! Turn out the guard!"

Powie! Spike Dillon, dropping to one knee, fired on the man, half seen in the dusk, who had taken his horse. Bent low in the saddle, kicking the pony to headlong speed, whipping him with the ends of his bridle reins, Sam heard the whistle of Spike's first bullet passing over his head. He could also hear the loud confusion as the whole camp came to life. Herd guards were shouting in the gloom, bunching up the mules. The sentries of the chain guard, strung around the wagons, were bawling back and forth. From the post of the main guard in the rear of the train Sam could hear a bugle bray the call to arms.

He dared not ride directly toward the mules. He didn't wish to stampede them, set the wagons down without pulling stock so near hostile Indians. He veered to his right, seeking to circle around the herd and its attending guards.

The pony picked up a sagebrush stub with a forefoot and almost pitched over on its spotted nose. Half thrown from the saddle, Sam hung to the reins while the pony struggled wildly to regain its balance.

A mounted guard loomed in the night, coming on the gallop. Sam kicked his mount so mightily in the ribs that he believed he had fractured a heel.

"Halt!" the guard roared. *"Halt!"*

Sam dared not halt. He ducked his head and belted his pony on through the tall sagebrush with the ends of the reins. The guard's gun blazed as he passed on the run. The blasting explosion, the red muzzle flash in the darkness, put terror into the Indian heart of Sam's pony.

The digger began running as though for first money in a Kentucky Derby. Sam crouched on the hurricane deck, hanging to the taut reins, letting the little animal work its stout legs like pistons.

He heard to his rear, another blast from the guard's gun, then a beat of hoofs. The fool was chasing him. Sam swung around in his saddle.

"Wagh!" he yelped, like a wolf, giving a fair imitation of a Sioux war whoop. "Wagh!"

That dread yelp checked the guard where perhaps a white man's gun would not have succeeded. For all the guard knew, Indians might be attempting to jump the herd. He did not wish to be lured into the prairie shadows where they could pull him off his horse and take his scalp. The guard reined in.

Finally clear of the camp and its guns, Sam checked his mount. He turned off toward the south-east in the general direction of Paint Rock Sinks. He dared not take any trail that a horse could travel easily in the night. He might encounter Canada Pete on his way to a rendezvous with the Kicking Horse, taking to the Sioux war chief the terms of whatever bargain he had struck with Chicago Jack.

Sam did not fear greatly that he would encounter hostile Indians. Only in emergencies did the warriors roam around at night. That was the dread season when ghosts walked. Warriors preferred to stay near their cheerful campfires at night. There were, of course, some exceptions. Warriors of great courage taking advantage of savage fear of the dark, sometimes stalked a rival band's camp and stole horses and occasionally women.

Figuring that he must cover at least thirty miles before he reached the Painted Rock country, Sam moved steadily on while darkness covered the earth. The wind carried a chilling bite, for it had switched to the north-east and was blowing down from the snowfields of the distant Big Horns. The moon would not rise for a couple of hours. A drift of clouds obscured the stars in the black sky.

Far off in the darkness Sam heard the melancholy calling of what he believed was a rain crow. And then, while he guided his pony through a patch of giant sagebrush that reached to his waist, he heard the hooting of an owl.

He reined down instantly. He dared not dismount. He was barely breathing. It might, of course, be an owl. But he could not forget that the hooting of an owl was the signal favoured by Canada Pete. And it was favoured because it was also the customary call of prowling Indians.

The owl hooted again. And this time, as though in answer, from some distant ridge enveloped in darkness, Sam heard the quavering howl of a coyote rise toward the stars. He felt little quivers of fear run up his backbone. He felt almost certain that a coyote wasn't howling.

Sam would have bet a stock of blue chips that it was some Indian buck over on that ridge answering the owl hoot signal with a coyote song. Perhaps they were passing Canada Pete through whatever scouting lines they had thrown out above the wagon train. Whatever the reason, it behove a lone white now to move with the utmost caution if he expected to die at a green old age with his hair straight.

Sliding gingerly from his saddle, Sam moved around to where he could keep a tight hold on the bride reins, and put a hand over the nose of his pony.

The hours of the night seemed to stretch out endlessly as Sam waited tensely in the sagebrush draw. But the owl—if it had been an owl—apparently had flown away in search of prey. The coyote no longer wailed from yon ridge. At last, Sam dared to move on. But for a time he stayed down in the draw, down where kindly shadows would hide him, where he could strike instantly for some hiding place if owls and coyotes became howling Sioux horsemen riding out of the night.

But although he felt the icy cold sweat of fear, he had made up his mind with a grim certainty. He would scout out the camp of the Kicking Horse. He owed that to his partners.

CHAPTER XVI

The moon rose above the dark hills, a pale and watery moon half shrouded by a drifting rack of clouds. But it offered a better light for the trail. The owls and coyotes were silent. Sam mounted the brown pony and took to the high ridges, knowing he must make better time if he hoped to arrive at Paint Rock Sinks before Canada Pete concluded his powwow with the Kicking Horse.

Knowing the Sinks, Sam decided that any camp would be near the only spring of good fresh water within many miles. He was passing now through a low country which had eroded away though the centuries under the continual punishment of sun and wind and frost. Soft earth had been washed down the draws. Only spectral shapes of hard bare rock remained, spires queerly shaped like the towers of ruined prehistoric cities, vague clumsy contours of rock that resembled coiled serpents and horned beasts.

If the sun had been shining, its rays would have revealed the raw slashes of colour in the broken walls that Sam was passing. Mineral of red and green and black could be easily dug out and pounded up with animal fat to form the body paint of Indians.

The red bands came here often to stage their feasts and dances, to secure the paint for the war path and the scalp trail. It was a haunt known to all tribes of the north-west, a site sacred to the medicine chiefs, seldow fought over by rival bands since battles here might anger the Wanka Tanka, the Mysterious ruler of the heavens.

As he crossed a plateau littered with broken rock, a distant thudding like far-off thunder reached Sam's ears. He halted his horse, sat listening for a moment. He was not listening to thunder. He heard the distant beat of a tom-tom. The council was in progress. Canada Pete had reached the Sinks, and was holding his powwow with the Kicking Horse.

Sam picketed the pony then unsaddled, before he made another move toward the camp. He wrapped his lanky form in the saddle blanket. If he should encounter some Indian boy nightguarding the pony herd, he could muffle his head in the blanket and pass himself off as an Indian.

But it was more likely that since this band was on the war path, the braves would not be burdened with more than their favourite war ponies. And these prized horses would be picketed out, near at hand, wherever their masters built their wickiups.

Sam ran the chance that Indian dogs might be with the band. It was the invariable custom of Indian dogs to bark at any white man who came near. But warriors seldom took dogs with them on a raid.

The greatest risk Sam ran, as he crept toward a rimrock which overlooked the big spring in Paint Rock Sink, was that he would encounter some Indian stationed as a guard to prevent any invasion of the council.

Muffled in his blue cavalry saddle blanket, Sam crawled to the rim. He lay flat on his stomach gazing down upon a scene of barbaric splendour. A blaze of light from the dancing flames of a huge fire at first dazzled him. The loud insistent beat of the huge war drum, the shrill cries of the painted singers who sat around it, boomed against his ears. He could hear the shrill piping of the tiny medicine whistles fashioned from the wing bones of birds with which dancers were carrying on some sort of ceremonial dance. He heard, too, the rattling of the medicine drums, and the deep-toned chorus of warriors seated around the council fire, singing to the boom of the drums and the dancers' whistles.

Sam found himself looking down upon a band of at least one hundred warriors. He counted a half-dozen naked braves squatting around the huge tom-tom fashioned from the fleshed skin of a buffalo and hollowed cottonwood log. A pole had been erected near the fire. From the top fluttered a black mat of long hair. A dozen warriors, naked except for paint and beaded breech clouts, were stamping around this pole, blowing their medicine whistles, flourishing knives and stone-headed war mauls.

This was the scalp dance with which the braves of the band were quickening their courage before nerving themselves for the main battle with the white soldiers in the fort, the *akicita owanka*. The soldier camp.

A half-moon of grim warriors sat around the fire and the pole, watching the dancers. They were not in full paint. Some wore blankets pulled up over their heads. There were others gaudily streaked in red and black and wearing eagle feathers in their coarse black hair.

The dancing and the savage music ended abruptly. The scalp dancers retired to the grim and silent crowd. A man stood up and walked out toward the pole. He wore a red Hudson Bay blanket. He let it drop to his shoulders. Sam saw that he was an old man with long white hair. He was waving an eagle plume fan as he began to harangue the council.

Sam caught enough of the Sioux words, the graceful hand signs, to understand that opinions were divided in this band. The Kicking Horse desired a big war. But this old man with the eagle fan—which marked him as a chief—was bidding the young men stay off the war path. They were brave, but the pony soldiers were many. They had wagon guns that were loud as thunder, and could blow up a man and a horse a long way off. If the Kicking Horse had a claim against the white men, let him go to the Indian agent and seek justice. Why send out runners to call on the Ogallalas, the Uncapapas, the Minneconju? Why draw warriors of these tribes into a war—a *kicizapi*—in which they would gain nothing but quick death?

Let these young men remember the time, not so many winters back, when just a few soldiers in the mountains above the

hated fort on Piney Creek had broken the might of Red
Cloud. The Sioux had thought the pony soldiers would be
armed with guns that must be muzzle-loaded. So they had
allowed the whites to fire, then had rushed them, expecting
they would take scalps before the *akicita* could reload. But
the walkaheaps—the infantry—they had a new sort of gun
which could be loaded swiftly from the rear end. They had
reloaded so swiftly that they had caught the charging Sioux
by surprise. They had cut them down as a boy slashes ripe
fruit off a choke-cherry tree with a lashing quirt. Ah, that had
been a sad and bloody day for Red Cloud.

When the old man ended his talk, and covered his head
with the end of his blanket, the Indians in the ring who were
not in paint uttered deep agreement. They had nothing to
gain in a big war. The Kicking Horse could not show them
where they would gain anything at all. Better to remember
the pipe of peace they had smoked at Fort Laramie in 1868
when they made their marks on the white man's talking paper.

But then a tall Indian in full paint strode to the centre of the
ring. He was a magnificent specimen of manhood, a good six
feet tall in his moccasins, hawk-faced. Upon his bare breast
was painted the outline of a bucking pony. Around his upper
right leg was knotted a bandage.

Sam knew that he was looking down upon the Kicking
Horse, the chief who desired a big war with the soldiers down
in the fort on the Platte. Here stood the leader of the scouting party that had jumped the beaver cache camp. That
scalp, dangling from the top of the pole, was the hair of Sam's
faithful Shoshone friend, the Buffalo Hump.

The war drum boomed. The painted scalp dancers sprang
forward. Warriors leaped up from the council ring, flashing
their weapons, saluting their war chief. A medicine man,
wearing the shaggy scalp of a buffalo, still adorned with the
polished black horns, led the frenzied scalp dance.

Sam gritted his teeth and clenched his hands as he saw
that the medicine chief wore the blue blouse of a soldier, a
blouse with the white chevrons of an infantry sergeant upon

B.S.—4*

the sleeves. And slanted around the medicine man's waist by a cord was a brass army bugle.

Here was the big medicine, the *wakan* of the Kicking Horse. The coat and the horn he had taken away from the *akicita*. It had gained him a victory in the mountains. He had taken the hair of a brave chief of the Snakes—the Shoshones.

The Kicking Horse raised his right hand. The tom-tom pounding ended abruptly. The dancers and the shouting warriors resumed their seats. Angrily, the Kicking Horse, with savage oratory, refuted the calm arguments of the old chief who did not desire a big war. The Washingtons had lied again to the Sioux. They had said they would not allow the long hairs to overrun the buffalo along the Powder River. But they had broken their word as they had before. The long hairs were like the swarms of grasshoppers that ate up the good buffalo grass. They would starve out the Indians. Now was the time to drive them east of the Big Muddy river. Let those of the Ogallalas and Uncapapas who did not wish to fight go to their camps and live like squaws.

"*Waxte!*" roared the warriors who were hot for war. "Good."

But the Kicking Horse would not depend upon words alone. He would show the big medicine he had lately acquired which would bring the Sioux a victory over the white *akicita*. He reached out his right hand and a warrior handed over a rawhide sheath. From it the Kicking Horse slowly drew a rifle. There was at first not a sound around the council fire. Savage eyes were centred on the shining gun, the *mazakan*.

The war chief raised it to his right shoulder. He slanted the barrel toward the heart of the fire. Then he began to raise the lever. He flashed six roaring shots; ripping tearing bullets that flung blazing embers around the council circle. Then he held the gun high over his head, a savage grin on his gaunt, paint-streaked face.

"*Wakan!*" he shouted. "*Mazakan wakan.*" The magic gun of the long hairs, the gun that could shoot as fast as a warrior could race the lever. He would see that the Sioux acquired

plenty of these guns if they would but fight. Armed with such
weapons, they could laugh in the faces of walkaheaps armed
with rifles that must be reloaded after each shot.

"*Waxte*!" roared the warriors. "Good! Good!"

Sam saw now that many of those who had not yet painted
for war had tossed aside their blankets. They could not with-
stand the temptation of securing a magazine rifle. They would
give a pony load of buffalo robes for such a gun. A beaver
pelt for each cartridge. They would even give up a favourite
wife for such a weapon. The magic gun. The *wakan mazakan*.

Then a white man stepped from the shadows into the firelight. The dancing flames glistened on his shaggy black
beard. There stood Canada Pete. He stood with folded arms
while the Kicking Horse explained that here was the good
friend who would furnish the warriors with the fast shooting
guns. A pony, laden with pelts, was led into the circle. This
indicated the price that Pete had set on a gun.

But when the Kicking Horse waited for agreement from
Pete, the smiling trader shook his head slowly. The warriors,
baffled, began to mutter angrily. But Pete spoke now,
smoothly. He desired a gift on the prairie from the brave
Sioux. He was a lonely man. He required a woman to tend
his fire and cook his meat. The Kicking Horse knew of such
a woman. Let the Sioux show their gratitude by giving Pete
this gift.

Frowning, the chief looked down upon the squatty shaggy
figure of the trader. But Canada Pete, knowing that he held
high cards since presumably he possessed a secret stock of
guns from which had come the chief's weapon, waited with a
smile on his lips. When the chief grunted that this had not
been in the original bargain, this gift on the prairie of a
woman, Pete answered that he would return many women to
the Kicking Horse. There was, in fact, a beautiful white
woman who would shine like the sun in the lodge of the great
chief. She had hair that was the red colour of the sun on a
frosty morning. She was from a far-off land called
Meesouree.

Sam gasped. The renegade was offering Jane Payne to the Kicking Horse!

The bargain was struck. A pony load of furs for a gun. The free gift on the prairie. The big drum boomed. The barbaric dancers circled the pole on which dangled the scalp of a brave enemy, a chief of the Shoshones.

A figure muffled in a blanket was led into the ring while Canada Pete stood waiting and grinning. Warriors streaked in red and black war paint whipped off the blanket while the medicine chief in the army coat capered, and attempted unavailingly to blow his bugle.

There stood the comely Night Star, the widow of Buffalo Hump. She was taller than most Indian women. Her figure was shapely, half revealed in the scanty wolf robe with which they had covered her. Brass wire bracelets flashed on her wrists. She wore anklets of wire around her slim ankles, and a necklace of white elk teeth around her graceful neck. Her blue black hair had been combed down smoothly and vermilion paint drawn along the centre parting. There was rouge on her smooth round cheeks, her full hips. She resembled some barbaric Mongolian princess of the distant land from which these Indians were said to have come in ages past. The firelight gleamed softly on her glistening smooth brown flesh.

Sam Sling's breath quickened as he looked upon the tempting splendour of the Night Star, this faithful woman who had resisted all amorous advances from white men in the winter camp, this squaw who had been true to her mate. Had she gone over to the enemy?

He could not tell. She had lived enough around the whites to know how to tempt a trader like Canada Pete. To gain her favours, Pete had betrayed the camp in the mountains, aided in the murder of her husband. She had been painted and adorned as the prize of the Kicking Horse. But Pete had won his point. She would be given to him as the chief's gift on the prairie, the token that the gun deal with Pete was *waxte*—good.

They would attack and attack along the river until Pete had arranged to deliver the guns at the crossing on the stream of the Wolf. But they must not bother the wagons. The vehicles were required to haul the guns and ammunition.

The drum boomed again as the Kicking Horse led the Night Star to Pete. The trader took her gleaming painted body in his arms.

Sick at heart, Sam Sling turned and crawled back to where he had tied his pony.

CHAPTER XVII

Sam Sling broke from the rough badlands hills above the broad Platte Valley when the sun was man high over the eastern divide. He figured that he was two hours behind usual riding time from the Paint Rock Sink to the head of Wolf Creek. But the tough brown pony was tired and hungry. He had delayed, back on the trail, before dawn, to water the horse and allow it to graze.

He told himself, as he checked for a look over the winding course of Wolf Creek, that he could do with a little breakfast himself. He grumbled at Spike Dillon because the latter had not tied a bag of emergency rations to his saddle. Sam had pulled his belt up to the last notch in what he termed a Spanish breakfast.

Since he had made the long lap of his ride during darkness, he had not encountered any roving Indians. But he forgot his hunger and became alert when he jogged out of the hills. Not far distant, he saw the dugouts of the Wolf Creek outpost from which Lieutenant Prime had drawn his command of mounted scouts.

Sam made a cautious circle around the location. He didn't wish to be jumped by some sentry, and then subjected to hours of cross-examination by whoever was in command. Captain Budhouse, his former company commander, was ten miles on at Cantonment Sparks with almost a battalion of infantry, four lettered companies. Budhouse should be informed immediately that the Kicking Horse had really picked up plenty of strength for attacks all along the river.

But Sam wasn't challenged at the outpost. Taking courage, he examined the desolate windbeaten array of roofed-over caves dug in a cutbank above Wolf Creek which had housed federal doughboys. All were now deserted. There were a half-dozen of these holes in the wall. But blankets had been taken from the crude, home-made board bunks, and Sam couldn't find so much as a can of bacon to take the wire edge off his appetite.

The brown pony fared better. A stack of wild hay had been shaped up a few yards from the edge of a small log shack that had served as the headquarters of the outpost commander. The provender had been hauled from Sparks to feed the mules and ponies of the mounted scouts. Indian diggers were unfamiliar with hay and oats, but the brown nibbled gratefully at the stack while Sam made his prowl.

An attempt had been made to link the outpost with Cantonment Sparks by a telegraph line but this had been given up as a failure. Roving Indians burned down the poles. They cut the wire. Since telegraph wire had a special magical meaning to them, they considered it big medicine and made bracelets and anklets for their squaws and themselves. Night Star had worn telegraph wire ornaments at the Paint Rock reunion with Canada Pete.

As Sam remounted and headed on toward the river, following the general course of Wolf Creek, he saw that some of the burned poles had been reset by repair patrols. As the charred ends had been chopped off, these poles were now quite near the surface of the earth. A man could stand on a saddle on a horse and reach the wire.

A quarter-mile south of the outpost, he swung over the Wolf Creek crossing, and paused to examine the ground. This was the spot which Canada Pete had named as the place where he'd turn over the fast-shooting rifles and ammunition to the Kicking Horse. Above and below, the creek cut its way between rather steep banks, but here a shallow gravel ford offered good footing for men and horses. South of the crossing, the road ran into a short narrow canyon that pierced a low range of hills. When Sam jogged through the canyon, he wrinkled his nose at the odour of something dead on the air, and saw two big turkey buzzards circle away from a carcass in the grass not far off the main trail.

He didn't particularly fancy examining the carcass on an empty stomach. But with Indians on the war path, he might find something of more serious import than a dead horse or game animal. He couldn't forget that his partners were abroad on this range. With the outpost deserted, there was always the chance that a traveller along the road would have his hair lifted by roving Sioux.

But Sam lingered only a moment over the buzzards' banquet. It was a dead pony, sprawled out, and so long dead that the body had swollen and the upper legs stuck into the air. Sam wondered what form of death had overtaken the digger but he didn't pause to make any close inspection. Too many buzzards and blow flies. He rode on.

Toward noon he came out on the Oregon Trail winding along the north side of the Platte River. He was now inside the trespass line run by the army against whites intruding on Indian territory. On flats that were muddy during stormy seasons, he saw a width of ruts of emigrants' wagon wheels a hundred yards wide where emigrants had turned off the main course to escape bog holes. Sam saw, too, the customary debris of the Oregon Trail, the empty bottles and barrels, old clothing, white bones of buffalo and work stock, rotting furniture cast off to lessen weight, a ragged dress once worn by a baby fluttering in the wind from a grey old sagebrush.

There were other signs too, along the trail, cairns of stones not far from the road, marking where rested men and women and children who had not lived to reach the promised land. Sam shook his head and rode on. These greenhorns, he reflected, would risk almost anything to lay hands on gold in

Montana or California. Of course, he was fair enough to admit, some had headed west seeking new homes. The transcontinental railroad now ran westward through the southern end of the territory, but plenty of covered wagons still stayed on the old trail, going as fast as a mule or an ox could walk from civilisation to the Pacific.

Sam's jaw tightened grimly when he came down to the grassy elbow on the river where Canada Pete had established his trading post. Pete had erected a couple of goodsized log shacks, using cottonwood logs cut along the nearby river. Around the buildings were arrayed round pole corrals, a big stack of wild hay, several dugouts, even a boarded-up shack in which Pete stored ice that he cut on the river in the winter. Pete had been here before the army established Cantonment Sparks, a mile east on the trail. He had been reckoned as a sharp dealer, but there had been no really black marks against his record, either with reds or whites.

Knowing that Pete had a cache of arms somewhere, Sam ran his glowering eyes over the post, wondering where the guns and cartridges would be hidden. In some clever place, undoubtedly. But no time now to make a search. Anyway, let the army take that end over.

Desiring to eat before he reached the cantonment, Sam tied up at the rack in front of Pete's main building. A four-horse outfit had made a halt for nooning. Two or three saddle ponies were also lined up along the rail. Sam's first glance at the riding stock was indifferent. Then his eyes narrowed. He moved over to one dust-caked Indian digger. This was the pony Shorty had topped on the wild ride for the top of the peak the last time Sam had seen him. No sign, though, of the horse Tom Bear Mouth had ridden.

For a moment elation swelled Sam's heart that his old partner had saved his hair and reached the river. Then his spirits fell. A reckoning was due with his partners, and he was never much of a man to mouth out excuses for neglect of duty.

The post door was wide open, for Pete believed in letting

it stay that way in summertime so that flies could not only enter but also drift out. A big round table near the greasy trading counter over which had passed a small fortune in buffalo robes and beaver pelts was ringed by several bearded men in trail rig. Sam saw a black jug on the table.

One man at the table reached for the jug as Sam entered. The rank odour of trade whisky, gurgling from the jug into a tin cup, smote Sam's nose. It reminded him of the smell of Sunset Liz's pain killer. Beyond the table, he saw Pete's wife, a quiet Indian woman, moving around back of the counter, waiting on trade, in the absence of her mate. She was called Little Bird, although she ran to fat. She was of the Ogallala Sioux, but she had been truly married to Canada Pete by a black-robed father several years before. This explained why Pete was regarded by the Sioux as safe to trade with.

Sam wasn't thinking about Little Bird. His eyes were hard on the man who was filling the tin cup. The man was Rocky Mountain Shorty. Shorty's garments were ragged and covered with trail dust. He looked as though he had just emerged from a sandstorm. He was mumbling to himself as he poured his drink. His hand shook so that he spilled whisky all over the table.

Another bearded man yelled boozily, "Go keerful, ol' man, with rotgut you ain't buyin'."

They were all, including Shorty, half drunk. Sam saw at once. He looked around for Tom Bear Mouth, but the Shoshone wasn't in sight.

In his cups, old Shorty was ordinarily a merryhearted man. But something today had soured him. When his drinking companion reproved him, even mildly, Shorty took offence. He staggered up from his chair, reached down, and whipped his long skinning knife from its bearded belt sheath. He seized the man who had bought the whisky by the end of his shaggy beard. He jerked the man's head forward. Shorty's eyes were glaring and red-rimmed. He rasped out that he could cut the throat of any man there who deemed him a cheapskate. It wasn't his fault, he lamented bitterly, that circumstances had broken him. He'd bought plenty of drinking whisky from Pete before this and they all knew it. Any more fool talk and he'd go to work with the skinning knife.

A man in a red shirt, across the table, unlimbered a six-shooter and lined on Shorty. "You drop that knife, you locoed old galoot," he wheezed, "or I'll drop you."

The man whose beard Shorty had seized sat in a paralysed fear, eyes popping like those of a big bullfrog. He dared not move or breathe.

Shorty was so deep in liquor that he didn't fear the drawn gun. He shrugged his scrawny shoulders, and tickled the throat of the bearded man with the edge of his knife.

"I'll have my steel into Jake here," he growled, "before you can pull off your iron!" Then, suddenly, his anger faded and maudlin sorrow overcame Shorty. Releasing the beard, he dropped into his chair. He shook his head and the tears rolled down from his rheumy eyes. But he didn't put up his knife. "They've all quit me," he moaned. "Boys—yuh jest can't blame me for bein' soured on men. I had two good pards—but they both turned down ol' Shorty. Wimmen was their curse, boys. Wimmen!" And sobs shook Shorty.

They forgot that he had just threatened to cut a friend's throat. They put up their guns, filled their cups, drank, and wept consolingly with Shorty. Even the man with the beard allowed huskily that he would have cut out his tongue if he had known Shorty would take his warning in an unfriendly way. In a moment, Shorty had thrown his arm around Jake's shoulder and was sobbing on his shoulder.

Sam stepped over gingerly and touched the old mountaineer on the sleeve.

"Hey, old man," he said huskily. "All your pards ain't quit you."

Shorty quit sobbing. His body tensed. For a long moment he said not a word to Sam. Then he came out of the chair as though a wasp had stung him. His eyes blazed with a mad red light. He poised the skinning knife for a thrust.

"Pard!" Shorty squalled. "You're a fine pard! Turned me and Tom down for a female! We both seen it from the butte. Soft on a female! By cracklin—" Shorty dived for Sam in an effort to seize him and drive the skinning knife into his breast.

It looked to Sam as though he'd be forced to knock out Shorty to save his life.

But Little Bird had been trained by her husband to handle tough customers. She came sidling around the end of the counter, reached up and tapped Shorty on the back of his narrow head with the wooden mallet with which bungs were started in barrels. Not a hard tap. An experienced snap in the right spot that took all the fight out of Shorty instantly. His eyes rolled back. His legs came apart at the knees, and he folded up. Little Bird, catching him expertly as he fell, lowered him to the floor. Sam bent and picked up the knife that had fallen from Shorty's hand.

Little Bird was dragging Shorty around the counter as Sam pulled out for the cantonment. Jake and the rest had resumed their singing and drinking.

The battalion of infantry was in tents along the river. Sam passed the picket lines and corrals where mules and ponies were cared for. There were two big stacks of hay near the round pole corral where mules and horses could be broken. Then came a log shack at the head of a long street of dingy wall tents. A brisk sentry in blue walked post in front of the building. The flag fluttered gently from the top of a pole.

This was cantonment headquarters. The sentry was a stranger to Sam. He gave his dirty buckskins, his greasy shock of black hair a wry glance but passed him into the shack. There was an outer office in which sat a fresh-faced young lieutenant back of a desk marked "Adjutant."

Sam gave his name and announced that he had a message for the cantonment commander. Vitally important. A door led to an inner room, and this door was suddenly flung open. Framed there stood a stocky, bald-headed man in a rusty blue uniform, with a shaggy, tobacco-stained, brindle moustache framing his hard, thin mouth. This was Captain Budhouse.

"Sling," snapped the captain, "you got the brass nerve of a river gambler to come here!" He turned to the adjutant. "Lieutenant," he ordered crisply, " call in the guard. Put this man under arrest. Throw him in the guard-house until further orders."

CHAPTER XVIII

Sam was carrying Shorty's skinning knife on his belt. At the captain's angry order, his own temper flared hotly for a moment. He dropped his hand to the knife haft, stepping toward the commander as he did so.

Budhouse misinterpreted Sam's instinctive reach for the knife as a hostile move, as did the young adjutant. The lieutenant came flying around the end of the desk, struggling with clumsy fingers to unsnap a pistol from his belt, bawling all the while for the guard. The captain backed into his office, warning Sam at every step that he must forget the knife and submit to arrest.

The adjutant freed his pistol and rammed the barrel against the small of Sam's back just as the sentry came plunging into the office with bayoneted rifle thrust forward for a quick jab. "Aw, fer criminy's sake," Sam said disgustedly, "put up your guns! If I'd aimed to kill Capt'in Bug—Budhouse, my steel woulda been in his neck afore he could spit. All I come here was to tell you the Sioux are shapin' up for a war. They got a chief called the Kickin' Horse. He's all fired up to hit the river most any time."

Budhouse, listening, frowned, and nodded to the adjutant. "Take away his knife. Then have the guard stand by, here in the outer office."

Sam passed over the knife.

Closing the door on the adjutant and the sentry, Budhouse sat down at his desk. Sam stood across from him, dead tired on his feet. Right hungry, too. This old man had been a captain for ten years, grown grey in the service. Drawing a captain's pay now for handling a major's job. He was like Rick Sling, who belonged heart and soul to the army. Budhouse had always had a high regard for Rick, boosted him to sergeant over Bootle.

"Well," Budhouse said curtly, "what's all this about the Kicking Horse?"

Sam told him. He included his belief that Canada Pete intended to deliver rifles and shells to the Sioux at Wolf Creek crossing within three days. Sam left out the part about the Night Star. That would only lead to complications bringing in the illegal beaver hunt and the ensuing fight.

For Sam still laboured under the impression that, once he had convinced the captain of his good intentions, he would be freed.

Budhouse jotted down a few notes while Sam talked. He unrolled and scanned a map of the country, pencil pointing out the various places mentioned by Sam. Then he leaned back in his chair, scratching his stubby moustache with one end of his pencil, and said, "Well, after all this, I reckon you think the army ought to pin a medal on you."

"Heck," said Sam, "I didn't set out to be no fool hero. Thought you should know about the Injuns."

"You spoke of being with that wagon train but you didn't have much to say about just *how* you happened to get there. The army's curious to know where you were about ten days back. If you'll give me a good fair answer to that, maybe I'll take more stock in your yarn about these war-dancing Sioux."

Sam frowned. If he told the truth, he must reveal that ten days ago he had been on trespass territory, happily trapping beaver with Shorty and Tom Bear Mouth, unaware that savage plans were afoot to rob and kill. But if he talked up now, he'd involve his partners. He had enough already to explain to Shorty and Tom without dragging the blamed army in on their tracks. So he stood silent.

Budhouse sighed. "Ten days ago," he explained, "the paymaster started from this post to pay off the half-company stationed at the Wolf Creek outpost. Those men—like the companies here—hadn't been paid for five months. Corporal Bootle drove the ambulance. A young bugler—who had been here on sick leave—rode in the seat with the corporal. The sergeant commanding the outpost, who had been here on some business about rations, rode ahead on his pony to scout out the road. Another mounted guard trailed the ambulance."

The captain paused and gazed out the dirty window. Then he resumed. "There was about five thousand dollars in gold coin in the chest inside the ambulance. We presumed the armed escort was heavy enough to see it through. We were wrong. A gang—some of them in paint and feathers like Indians—jumped the outfit in a little canyon this side of Wolf Creek."

Sam, listening intently, nodded. That was where he had smelt and seen the dead pony.

"They stampeded the mule team, upset the ambulance. They killed the paymaster, the young bugler, and the rear guard."

"What about the sergeant?"

"Corporal Bootle got into the brush. He said later that the last he saw of the sergeant, he was galloping away from the scene as fast as his horse could gallop."

"Goin' for help to the outpost," Sam said, "or—"

"Or saving his own hide. That's what Corporal Bootle said."

"I seen a dead horse in that canyon today. Dead some time. Reckon it belonged to one of the dead men, rear guard or sergeant. Carcass used up some by buzzards, but pony had been a roan."

"The sergeant isn't dead. He was riding that roan. He came into the outpost afoot. He swore that they had hit his pony in the neck with an arrow. The animal bolted. He was forced to shoot it to stop it. Bootle swears the sergeant is a liar."

"Bootle never could drive mules," Sam said, pondering. "Reckon that's why the army always had him doin' it. Like the wagon train—"

The captain cut him short. "Forget Bootle. The gang— white men or Indians—they got the five thousand in gold. One of them left forty dollars in gold to pay for a military funeral for the paymaster."

"How about the enlisted men, the bugler and the rear guard?"

"They knew the army would bury them free of charge." The captain added, "They took the bugle young Jones was carrying. And they also stole the blouse off the back of the sergeant's saddle after he had killed his pony."

Sam's eyes glinted. He leaned on the desk. "It's my guess that the Kicking Horse and Canada Pete were in on the hold-up. At that Paint Rock shindig, the Injuns sported a bugle and an army blouse as strong medicine."

"Indians," the captain said curtly, "aren't much interested in gold money."

Sam knew this for a fact. Money meant little to wild Indians. Being savages, they took more stock in goods they could see. They seldom took money for their pelts from traders. They were paid off directly in blankets, guns, paint and beads and the like. Knowing nothing about money values, they were cheated most of the time but, happily, didn't know it.

So the captain didn't lay the blame for the raid on Indians. He intimated that white renegades, disguised as Indians, had robbed the paymaster.

"Canada Pete," Sam cried. "He organised that raid. Then, later, he traded the pony soldier coat and bugle to the Sioux, makin' 'em believe it was heap strong medicine. You round up this Canada Pete and you'll have the he dog of all this trouble that's started to pop."

"Pete has been a good friend to the army. Often assisted us with valuable information."

Sam growled. He had also succeeded in pulling the wool over army eyes.

Captain Budhouse ran his shrewd eyes over Sam's dirty buckskins and moccasins. "Now you're the young Sling who goes in for Indian clothing and ways. You quit the army for that. I'll bet you've wore moccasins so long you toe in when you walk. And if they put army brogans on your feet again, you'd develop broken arches from the high heels."

"Now listen, Captain."

Budhouse pushed back his chair. He stood up. "After the robbery, I gave orders to arrest all suspicious characters who could pass as Indians but couldn't tell a good story of where they were ten days ago."

Now Sam understood why Spike and the rest had scorned him. They were under orders not to talk about the murder and robbery. Even Bootle hadn't talked. Finding him in suspicious territory, garbed like an Indian, likely the soldiers had decided that he was one of the gang. Since Sam wouldn't tell where he had come from, vague suspicion had grown into a certainty.

Sam shrugged and nodded. Now he was all fixed up. The army hated him as a payroll robbery suspect. Shorty and Tom believed he had quit them for a female. The female sniffed at sight of him because she believed he had flirted with Sunset Liz and her girls.

"If that's all, Captain, I reckon I'll be goin'."

The captain nodded. "Go right ahead."

Sam turned, repressing the old soldier instinct to salute the captain. He opened the door and stepped out into the adjutant's office.

He stopped. His jaw gaped. His eyes popped.

Three belted soldiers of the guard stood waiting for him with fixed bayonets. The corporal in command was his old friend, Jimmy Kerry.

"Confine him," the smooth-faced adjutant ordered.

Kerry regarded Sam with stony eyes. "Will you come peaceful," he asked, "or shall we put you in irons?"

Sam stared back at his former comrade's harsh face, accusing eyes. His whole world had now turned upside down.

"How do you feed in the mill?" he drawled.

"You ought to know. You spent enough time in it."

"Hash, I hope. I could stand some hash. Let's go."

They marched him from the shack, past the tent which housed the guard, and into another flimsy shack which served as the guard-house. An armed sentry unlocked the door. They thrust Sam inside and slammed the door on him. He heard the key grate in the lock. The light was dim in here, since only one small window had been cut in the wall. That was high up, and barred to boot. There were large cracks in the walls through which some light slanted, for green, whip-sawed lumber always warped, out here on the plains.

"Shucks," Sam said, "who wants to get out? They'll be blowin' mess call in another hour."

He saw three men seated in the gloom on the double-tiered bunks across the room. Coming in from the sun, he couldn't recognise them at first. Assuming they were fellow-prisoners, penned up for minor breaches of discipline, he padded across the room.

Then he halted. The grin froze on his hairy face. He knew these prisoners.

They were—reading from right to left—Spike Dillon, Private Huffenberger, and his own brother, Rick Sling.

For their part, they never arose. They sat in hard-jawed silence, watching him with eyes that looked as level and dangerous as the aimed barrels of cocked rifles.

CHAPTER XIX

Huffenberger, swinging his big feet from an upper bunk, dropped to the dirt floor. Red with anger, he advanced on Sam with his fists up.

"All I ask," sputtered Huffenberger, "is one good punch at that grinnin' mugg of your'n."

Spike Dillon, seated on the edge of the lower bunk beneath the private, dodged his head as Huffenberger descended. Then he jumped up and walked toward Sam, his dark face twisted with anger. "I'm the oldest soldier here," he said coldly to Huffenberger. "I rate the first punch at him."

Sam slowly backed up. Of course he knew why they were here. But it appeared odd that they had reached the cantonment before his arrival. Prime would have only one recourse after Sam's escape: to put the corporal and the private under arrest for allowing it.

All that broke up an immediate fight was the interference of Rick Sling. He stepped between the two enraged soldiers and Sam. He looked his brother over bleakly but didn't extend his hand.

"You still seem to have your old-time ability for getting into trouble," he observed. "Haven't seen you since your discharge, four years ago. And when I do, danged if it isn't in jail."

"It's a poor place for a family reunion, I'll admit," Sam answered, "but you seem to be in the same place yourself. Last I heard of you, you sported a sergeant's chevrons and were headed for top when old McNeal retired. Now you're in the hole with me."

Spike attempted to push past Rick Sling but the sergeant thrust him aside. Rick was a bulky man, with iron-grey hair, face deeply wrinkled from years of service, and browned the colour of an old saddle from western sunlight. A strong hard man, the perfect type of the old army redneck. Huffenberger, still ready to fight, tried to go around Rick's other flank but Rick didn't waste a hand on him. He merely blasted a harsh order: "Get back to your bunk."

Huffenberger looked offended but he retreated as commanded.

"I suppose you know why they confined you?" Rick asked.

"Near as I can make out, I happened to be about fifty miles north of Wolf Crick when a jag of army pay was lifted and some soldiers killed. Since I dress like an Injun—like about nine-tenths of the civilian inhabitants of this territory —the army figures maybe I helped out on the deal. Captain Bughouse—"

"Call him by his right name," growled Rick.

"I call things as I see 'em, Rick. I'm not in the army now. I make a ride to let the army know the Kickin' Horse and the Sioux are painted for war. So they slam me in the mill."

Spike Dillon cut in, speaking between his teeth. "The captain forgot to say that you'll be charged with horse stealing. Government property. My horse. Soon as I can sign the charge that I identified you as the thief. You know how a guilty horse thief rates in this territory, even among civilians. You'll be lucky if you make the pen. They might take you away from the army and hang you."

Sam shook his head. There was no answer to Spike's charge. He had stolen a pony. Of course, he hadn't stolen it for personal profit. He believed he was doing the army a service. Perhaps he should've consulted with Lieutenant Prime. But he felt that Prime wouldn't have understood.

"Well," Rick interrupted his thoughts, "talk up. What about this pony stealing? And why in the world come in when you knew you'd be arrested?"

"It's a danged long story," said Sam. "When do we eat?"

"You don't eat," growled Spike. "Not with us."

"Forget this kid stuff," Rick said impatiently. "The guard'll stop any fightin' in here."

"I still say this buzzard don't eat with us," Spike insisted stubbornly. "You ain't issuin' orders no more, Rick. You've lost your chevrons."

"I'm confined," Rick grated, "but I'm not busted. A good man gave me those chevrons. It'll take good men to take 'em away."

"A general court-martial," sneered Spike. "Cowardice."

Rick swung around. He swung a punch for Dillon's chin but Spike dodged. In so doing, he came within range of Sam's right fist. A red blur of anger had blinded Sam when he heard his brother termed a coward. Sam swung from belt level, clicking his haymaker off Spike's jaw. Spike sagged at the knees. He wasn't knocked out but he sat helplessly on the floor, gasping for air.

Sam's quick rage faded as quickly as it had arisen.

"I ain't particular who or what I eat with," he announced, blowing on his knuckles. "But I'll tell the world that I eat when mess call goes if I have take this mill apart."

Rick shrugged and walked back to his bunk. "Thanks for steppin' in," he said, over his shoulder. "Of course, Dillon wasn't lookin' at you when you hit him."

Sam let that pass. He saw a stool on the far side of the room and went over and sat on it. Spike got up and staggered groggily to his bunk, rubbing his jaw. Huffenberger sat on the top one, dangling his feet, and growling deep in his throat. Rick rolled a smoke and watched his younger brother in a sort of cold remote silence.

Mess call went, and, soon after, a can of stew, hard tack, and a big pot of black coffee refreshed the prisoners. Corporal Kerry came in with the man off kitchen police who carried the provisions. He issued eating gear, for confined men weren't allowed to keep such things in the guard-house. They might dig out with spoon or stab a sentry with a general issue knife or fork. The army provided for all contingencies.

Sam ate until he felt as puffed up as a buffalo bloated on green greasewood. He stretched out his long legs and fumbled around in his possibles pouch for his old black pipe and the tiny hunk of twist tobacco that he had hidden from Shorty when smoking ran low in the hills. He filled up the pipe, stepped over, and lit it at the lantern which Kerry had placed on the centre table, then resumed his seat. Here, his mind somewhat at ease since he had been fed, he emptied his possibles pouch hunting for something that might aid him in a break-out. The guard had taken away all dangerous articles such as Shorty's knife and a block of sulphur matches. But they hadn't lifted the arrow head which Shorty had taken out of Sam's side.

Sam looked at the gracefully fashioned but barbed flint head. A portion of the shaft was fastened to it. Sam recalled Shorty's remark that the shaft marks might provide Tom with a clue to the identity of the warrior who had used it. Warriors often put marks on arrows to prove ownership. That way they could claim credit for killed wild game or men.

Rick laid his eating tools on the table and stepped over. He asked Sam where he had picked up the arrow head. Sam gave him a vague answer. A Sioux had taken a shot at him. He had kept the broken off head and shaft, hoping by the marks to prove ownership.

"So they put marks on them, hey?" Rick asked. "I had heard of that." He held out a broken shaft end to his brother. "You sabe Injun stuff pretty good. Take a look at this."

The marks were rather obscured by dried blood, but Sam washed some of it off with cold coffee. He said finally that he'd bet the same warrior had once owned both arrows. He *knew* that his arrow had been fired by an Indian with the band of the Kicking Horse.

"Then," Rick said, "it was that bunch of reds that jumped the paymaster. I don't know how much the captain told you about the deal, but you've probably guessed by now that I was the sergeant whose pony was stampeded. Bootle claims I ran away."

Sam hadn't known when they put him jail but he had suspected when Spike spoke of a charge of cowardice. The meeting with Rick had not been an affectionate one, but Sam would fight any man in the world who called old Rick a coward. He got up and said as much. He also added that this was another example of army dumbness, the captain charging Rick with being a coward.

Bootle's the one making the charge," Rick said grimly.

"It's the captain who is standin' up for me. He'll probably be forced by army regulations to prefer charges on Bootle's say so, but he'll go to bat for me before the court. I'm dependin' on his help." He took another look at the arrow portions. "This may help out my case when I show 'em to the captain and he hears your story."

Spike, listening to the talk, jeered, "Best thing you Slings can do is tell where you hid our pay."

Sam started across the room, hot to take on Spike. Spike, just as willing, jumped up to meet him. Huffenberger slid down eagerly, to get in on the fight. But Rick Sling again intervened. This time he held off his hot-eyed younger brother. It was now Sam who yearned to wipe the nasty grin off Spike's swollen face.

"There's some truth to what Dillon says," Rick said wearily. "Fightin' won't help. It's up to us Slings to produce the gold to prove to these iron-headed soldiers we didn't steal their pay money."

"Us?" asked Sam.

"Sure."

Rick painted a black picture for the Sling family. Describing his part in the payroll robbery, he told Sam he had been riding ahead of the ambulance when he heard the yells and gunfire of the attack. He attempted to turn back, but a whizzing arrow, striking his roan pony in the neck, stung the little horse to madness. It stampeded, running out of control. Drawing his pistol, Rick shot it to check its wild flight. Thrown off, stunned, he crawled into cover. Three painted raiders, galloping past the dead horse, halted. One dismounted and took his blouse off the saddle.

"When it was all over," Rick went on, "I staggered back to the wrecked ambulance. Bootle had taken to the brush. Only man left alive. He accused me of runnin' away. We started afoot for the outpost. I wanted to show him how the pony had been shot. He wouldn't believe me. I cut off the arrow head shaft thinkin' it might be evidence. Got to the outpost, sent word to the captain. He relieved me of command. When Bootle accused me of bein' a coward, he confined me.''

With the arrest of Sam, suspicion had been strengthened that perhaps the Slings had actually been involved in the raid. When Sam stole a horse to escape, Prime believed it so important that he sent a detail of scouts riding through the night to the cantonment with this new information for the commander. Spike and Huffenberger were sent in with the detail as prisoners for neglect of duty.

"The whole deal revolves around Canada Pete," Sam said. "He's mixed up in all this. He's played a smooth game until now with all of us, trappers and army alike. But he gave himself away when I spotted him dickerin' with the Kickin' Horse and the Sioux.''

"Trouble with that is," said Rick, "that nobody but you saw this dickerin' around. You'll have to tell the captain how you come to be prowlin' around in Injun country when the soldiers caught you.''

"They didn't catch me, exactly. If it hadn't been for that fool of a Bootle—" He frowned and shook his head. "Bootle hates you Rick. You're in his way. He wants your stripes. I'd like to hang around and talk some with the captain. But he'd better hold an early powwow with me.''

"Why?''

"Because I'm figurin' to bust out of this snap 'most any minute.''

CHAPTER XX

The night passed, and it was well past noon of the next day when the Slings marched, under guard, into the captain's office.

Sam was amazed to find Jane Payne, her fat old guardian, Barberry, and Lieutenant Prime in waiting. But more surprising was the presence of Canada Pete. Sam turned with a scowl, on the trader, but Pete eyed him with a winning smile.

"You renegade," Sam growled.

Captain Budhouse interrupted sharply. "Sit down, Sling. And keep your mouth shut until you're asked to say something. I'm conducting a sort of inquiry here into some serious charges that have come up. One—for instance—against you, charging you with escaping arrest and stealing a government-owned horse to get away on. So sit down!"

Sam sat down gingerly on a stool near the door. He didn't answer the captain. He kept his glowering gaze on Canada Pete. The trader, for his part, sat at ease, vastly unconcerned.

Prime soon supplied the reason for the trader's return to army favour. Pete had caught up with the wagon train after the first forced night march, shown a short-cut to the lieutenant by which ten miles of distance had been cut off the hard drag to the river. The various owners and their outfits were now safely camped near Pete's post. The army was deeply indebted to Pete for his assistance.

"So far as your charges go of this man having a store of rifles and shells on hand for sale to hostile Indians," Captain Budhouse said to Sam, "I'll add that a detail searched his property yesterday. No such articles were discovered."

Sam listened, then drawled, "Can I talk now?"

"If you have anything to say."

"You never rated me high as a soldier, Captain. But in four years of service under you, I was never accused of bein' a liar. You're callin' me a liar now. I don't know where he cached his rifles and such, but he'll get 'em to the Kicking Horse somehow. That's the deal I heard, and I told you straight."

The captain frowned, looking from Sam to the smiling trader. Then he rubbed his stubby moustache with his pencil point. "A man might change after he leaves the service," he said slowly. "Other things have come up lately such as the raid on the paymaster's outfit. Both you Slings are poor men. You'd be in a position to stage a mock Indian attack to throw off suspicion. Five thousand dollars in gold is a lot of money to poor men. A clever yarn to divert suspicion to some other man might be part of your plan."

Sam made no answer. His temper was rising and he knew that if he talked, he'd have the captain calling out the guard. The interruption of the captain's musing speculations came from an unexpected source. From Miss Jane Payne of Missouri. She snapped to her feet, thrust out her dimpled but firm chin, and said to Budhouse:

"It is amazing how ridiculous men can be. Just because you arrest a man fifty miles north of your silly trespass line, you accuse him of robbery and murder."

"We haven't accused him of that. So far it is just horse stealing. We'll charge him officially with that when Corporal Dillon signs the affidavit that he recognised Sling as the thief who took his pony."

"Don't put me off, Captain. I heard most of the story about these Sling brothers when our train came in this morning. All the teamsters were talking about it. Said the army was about to accuse one of its trusted sergeants of cowardice because his horse got stampeded by Indians and ran away with him." Her eyes flashed. "When I heard the name of the man who accused him of cowardice, I knew it was a lie."

"The man who laid the charge was Corporal Bootle. He was driving the mules on the raided ambulance," Budhouse rapped out. His eyes narrowed. "I'd prefer, Miss Payne, that you confine your talk to actual experience. We are not dealing with sentiment just now."

She sniffed. "Sentiment, shucks. Bootle knows very well that mules and horses frighten easily in an Indian attack. I also know it, because I was riding with Bootle a few days ago when just such a thing happened. I came here today to tell you that if it hadn't been for Sam Sling, the Indians would have had my hair, and also that of your lying corporal." She shrugged her shoulders, turning toward the door. Sam was listening to her with a proud grin on his face.

Jane flushed and tossed her head. She laid a hand on the door knob, but Prime sprang forward to open the door for her. She tossed back to the captain the scornful remark that no cold-blooded bandit in his right senses would have jumped into a fight with Indians to save a strange girl and a soldier. It was unthinkable.

"He saved you, Miss Payne," growled the captain. "Naturally you are moved by kindly sentiments toward him."

She flashed Sam a glance as she stepped like a queen through the door. "I entertain no kindly sentiment," she allowed, "toward a man who thinks I'm a Missouri cornfed."

She went out into the adjutant's office, escorted by the attentive lieutenant. The captain sat scratching his whiskers with his pencil. Canada Pete was grinning widely. Sam Sling sat slumped in his chair with jaw hanging on his chest.

But Jane got no farther than the outer office. The sentry backed in, seeking to disengage himself from a rumpled up old man who clung to his neck like a tree sloth. It was Rocky Mountain Shorty and he was insisting loudly that he be allowed to talk to the captain.

"Take your hands off'n me, you old drunk," raged the sentry. "I tell you the captain's busy."

The adjutant pushed in to quiet Shorty, but the mountaineer, releasing his hold on the sentry's neck, reached out and pulled the adjutant's nose. "All you brass buttons can't keep me quiet!" he snarled. "I ain't drunk none. I'm a freeborn 'Murican citizen, and gotter right to see any danged officer I want to. Taxpayer, by cracklin'!" And he pulled the nose of the adjutant a second time.

Budhouse stormed from his office followed by the Slings, Canada Pete, and the girl's fat guardian.

"Take that drunk down and throw him in the guardhouse!" the captain thundered. He turned on the sentry and the adjutant. "What do you mean, allowing this commotion around headquarters?"

The angry sentry tried to apologise. The adjutant couldn't speak because he had just released himself from Shorty and was feeling with both hands for his tweaked nose.

"Captain Budhouse," Sam broke in worriedly, "he don't mean nuthin'. Just on a spree."

Shorty wheeled around and took a flying punch at Sam. "Budhouse!" he bawled. "Call him by his right name. Bughouse! Old Bughouse. They're all Bughouse. All these whippersnappers runnin' honest citizens south of the Platte, makin' pets of the danged Sioux. All Bughouse!"

Prime assisted the sentry to quiet Shorty. Sam stepped in to help Shorty. A rough-and-tumble scrimmage ensued.

The guard came on the run. Shorty and the two Slings were forthwith hustled back to the guard-house.

Once the door had been locked, Sam turned stormily on his old partner. "Now you've shore played the fool. Gettin' throwed in jail about time I got ready to break out and join up with you and Tom." He advanced on his old partner, who was doing a stomping variety of Indian corn dance in the middle of the room, and chanting like an Indian.

"Hi yah yah yah! Hi yah yah yah!"

"Quit corn dancin', you old drunkard! You smell like a distillery! Quit it, I say."

When Sam took Shorty's arm, intending to help the old fellow over to a bunk where he could sleep it off, Shorty flung his arms around his neck and broke into maudlin tears. Between sobs, Shorty whispered into Sam's ear, "Help me play out the hand! Tom's back. We'll beat the army yet."

Then Shorty's strength seem to fade. He subsided limply in Sam's arms. Sam picked up the scrawny old frame, clad in dingy buckskins, and toted it to the nearest empty bunk. He bent over Shorty, straightening out his legs and shaping a pillow for his head. Shorty's eyes were wide open, entirely sober, and he was whispering, so faintly that Sam could barely hear him.

"At dusk," Shorty cautioned. "Red Dog and Jake and the boys'll make believe they're a bunch of Injuns attackin' the post. That'll attract the attention of the guard. Then Tom'll fasten one end of a long string of mule trace chains to the bars in the window. One good pull by four mules, druv by Red Dog, and we'll pull out the hull back wall of this jail.''

Rick stepped up as Shorty quit talking.

"What's he saying to you?" Rick asked.

"Aw, just drunken gibberish!"

"You've got some deal ribbed up," Rick insisted. "He was whisperin' to you. I just picked up the last few words. Somethin' about pullin' out the back wall of this place."

Sam laughed and looked around the room. "Now how in the world would we do that? Sentry walkin' post outside this door. Post of the main guard next to us on the line. Only one window and that high up. Bars in it to boot."

"A man," Rick answered, after examining the situation, "could drag one of these double-decker bunks over and stand on the top one to reach the window. If he had some sort of tool—hack saws or somethin'—he could then cut out the bars so he could squeeze through the window." Rick turned with sudden decision to Dillon. "Come on, Corporal," he commanded. "Shorty's got somethin' hid on him to break out with."

"The guard already searched him," Sam said. "All they got was a bottle of rotgut."

"We'll search him again," said Rick. "You two hombres aren't leaving here tonight."

Rick started for Shorty's bunk. But Sam seized his brother by the shoulders. He swung him around and stared into his set face. "You mean that you'd try to keep us from makin' a break?"

"Sure," snapped Rick.

"But Bootle's accused you of bein' a coward. You're in this mill tonight. And old Bughouse talked about us bein' involved in that pay robbery. Yet if you had the chanct for a bust-out, you wouldn't take it." Sam reddened with anger. He shook his brother savagely. "Dang you and your blamed army. Dumb until you die. Why, a court-martial might find you guilty. You know what they can do to a soldier who runs away from the enemy."

"Yes. They can sentence him to be shot to death by musketry," Rick answered.

"You'd stay and take your chances!"

"I put in the best part of my life in the infantry, Sam. What I got, the army gave me. It ain't much. But until now, I've been respected by some darn good men. And one of 'em—this one you call Bughouse—he puts a sergeant's chevrons on me. They haven't taken 'em away yet. They can't do that until a court finds me guilty."

"So you're stayin'? Trustin' in your luck. Prayin' Bughouse'll help you."

"Not prayin'. Stayin' because I am innocent. Stayin' because I respect myself. Stayin', too, because if I did go over the hill tonight, they'd be dang sure that I was guilty from start to finish." Rick jerked away from Sam's clutch. He walked over to Shorty's bunk and grabbed the old man by the moccasins. He snapped to Dillon, "Help me search him, Corporal."

Spike snarled, never moving, "I'm not taking orders from you. Not while we're both under arrest."

Rick gave a heave that jerked Shorty from the bunk and flung him to the floor. Then he turned on the corporal. He ripped out army language that made Huffenberger's eyes pop, and wound up by rasping, "I'm still a sergeant. I'm pullin' my rank on you, Corporal. But if you don't help, I'll do more than that, I'll break your neck with my bare hands." He waited a moment, hands planted on his hips.

Spike stood up slowly. He was, first of all, an old soldier and a corporal to boot. Rick was the sergeant. He growled sullenly, "All right. What do I do?"

CHAPTER XXI

While Rick pulled rank on Spike, Shorty sat up indignantly, rubbing his back-side where his old bones had been jarred by hitting the hard-packed dirt floor. He still maintained a pretence of being drunk until Rick said sharply, "Stow that, you old bum! I've handled too many drunk soldiers in twenty years service to be taken into camp by you." He eyed Dillon. "You and Huffenberger stand off Sam while I take this faker apart."

Sam, watching Dillon swallow his anger and take orders from a man he mistrusted but must still respect because he was a sergeant, shook his head in amazement. He was more surprised when Huffenberger, another of the soldiers who had lost their pay and been convinced that Rick had taken part in the raid, slid from his bunk and stepped to Dillon's side.

There was something, after all, to being a soldier. There were a lot of dumb things about the old army, the way they did things backwards, starved out and missed their pay. But when it came down to bedrock, they stood together. They respected one another above personal hatred and envy and greed. The Bootles were exceptions.

Dillon was old in the service, Huffenberger young. But they swallowed their anger and stood shoulder to shoulder at Rick's command.

Sam possessed nothing to fight with but his fists. But here was the stool against the wall. He bent and picked it up. He gripped it by one leg and poised it, shoulder high. Now there was a grim smile on his lips and a light in his eye. He stood, with his legs widely braced, and his black hair falling to his buckskin-covered shoulders in wild disarray.

Huffenberger breathed hard through his big nose. "Sarge," he said huskily, "he's apt to brain me with that stool. We can call for the guard."

Rick laughed grimly. "Huff." he drawled, "you won't get hurt it he hits you on the head. But watch out for your feet. Remember what Stonewall Jackson said about the infantry. They got to take care of their feet."

Then Rick stepped out to meet Sam.

"Put down that stool, Sam. In the final windup, the army gives every man a break."

"Sky pilot talk," sneered Sam.

Old Shorty dropped his hands to his side. He had quieted down. He stepped out to the centre of the room. He called to Sam in a weary way, "Sam—they hold the high cards on us. Put down the stool."

"I'll stay with you, Shorty, until the last dog is hung."

"I know that, son. But a danged passel of beaver ain't worth all this." Shorty stepped nearer to where he could talk to Rick. "We didn't like the danged army trespass rules. We don't like 'em *yet*. We figured it would be easy to lift a few prime pelts from the Sioux."

"I figured it, Shorty," Sam said bitterly, "and I've cussed myself ever since."

"We was all in it with you. Tom Bear Mouth and Buffalo Hump and the Night Star, they figured they had rights above army rules because they were Shoshones who had once trapped in that part of the Big Horns. Times has changed, Sam," Shorty wagged his head sadly. "Fellers like you and me must also change or pull out. The army come here to set up civilised rules for folks that are different from us and the Injuns. Folks like those greenhorns you see in the wagon trains. Maybe their rules are the best now. We can see what happened when we busted 'em. A good man dead, his wife bad hurt, you and me in the army jug."

"Tom Bear Mouth's gone, Shorty. Maybe scalped."

"Tom come in. That's why I'm here. He slipped away, while you was gone, to scout the Sioux. He spied on a big powwow in Paint Rock. He saw a war dance there. He wanted to kill the Kicking Horse or Canada Pete but had no chance. Besides—"

Sam and the three soldiers were listening intently to the sad old mountaineer as he lamented the free days that were gone.

"What about Tom?" asked Sam, sensing something unsaid about the Shoshone's scouting of the Paint Rock powwow.

"He couldn't stay for stray scalps, Sam. His sister got away toward dawn. From the wickiup of Candy Pete. Pete had felt so good he took too much of his own trade whisky. Tom caught the Bright Star as she was kneeling under the stars ready to bury a knife in her heart. He brought her in. She's a shamed thing, Sam. She won't talk or eat or anything. We got her cached out in the hills. Got to keep her away from knives.''

"She acted like she had gone sweet on Pete," said Sam.

"He forced her. That's all, Sam. He wanted her so bad he framed that raid on the beaver camp. They got her before she could kill herself. They had jumped poor Buffalo Hump when he went down for water. She had no chance. The Sioux told her that Pete killed her husband. They wouldn't lay a hand on her, for she was the wife of a brave man. But they wanted rifles so bad from Pete that he took a free hand with her. She thought, until the last, that she could get away and tell us. But she had no chance. She acted willin' at the powwow because she wanted to get Pete drunk so's she could steal his knife and kill herself. She would have turned the trick if Tom hadn't found her.''

The stark tragedy of the Indian woman's life turned the listeners cold. They could see that scene under the pitiless stars with the Night Star kneeling in the sagebrush ready to drive her betrayer's knife into her broken heart. The silent approach of her brother, who gave up any hope of instant revenge so that he could save his pitiful sister.

Shorty pushed aside his hunting shirt, revealing his ribby middle. His buckskin pants were held up by a rawhide belt. He laughed and unlooped it. When it was unwound, it reached out for at least ten feet.

"My weapon," he laughed. "The fool guard who searched me figured it some sort of outlandish belt favoured by us mountaineers. Of course, he never knew that I could slip it between the bars and lower it so Tom could tie the end of the trace chains to it. Then I could pull up the chain and make a hitch on the window bar. After that, the fake Injun alarm to upset our guards. Then Red Dog and his mules would pull down the wall.''

The guard-house had grown shadowy. The monotonous

pacing of the sentry outside the door accompanied the recital of Shorty. The plan of escape, framed by the trappers and mule skinners, had been a wild one. But it might have succeeded. There were low hills in the rear of the camp covered with sagebrush. Four mules could be brought near the back of the building after dusk if the guard's attention could be turned in another direction by an apparent Indian attack. This building was flimsy, built of green, warped lumber.

"It might've worked," Rick Sling said, nodding wisely. He looked at Shorty with a kindlier eye. "You still smell like a distillery," he went on, "but maybe I've been wrong about you."

"Save it," said Shorty. "You and me lives different lives. If we get out of this deal without bein' set by the danged army to make little rocks out'n big ones, we'll go our separate ways. Folks say there's still room west along the Rockies. Army ain't strong there yet. Time they get there," Shorty smiled faintly and touched his forelock, "some danged Ute or Nez Perce'll likely have his hair."

"They'll have mine too," said Sam Sling. "Where you go, Shorty, I side you."

"No pard," said Shorty. "Your brother's always been right about you. You've had your fling now. But you're young. The West is growin' up fast. Stay here and grow with it, Sam." He stuck out his horny hand. "Tonight, kid, we split the blankets."

"No!" Sam vowed. "No."

Shorty shook his head and grinned. "By cracklin'," he drawled, "while I was huggin' that guard in the captain's office, I couldn't help seein' that pretty gal, Sam. She sure kept her eyes on you. She's the female you saved, Sam. Stay with her and grow up with the West." He winked.

Soon the guard would enter with the lantern for it was nearly dusk.

"She don't like me," growled Sam. "I called her a corn-fed."

Suddenly Shorty ended his soft talk. He turned his head

B.S.—5*

toward the door. The pacing of the sentry could no longer be heard. Somewhere, far off, there was a dim sound like the splashing of water, then a faint rumble as of drums rolling.

Sam and the soldiers, not gifted with the keen ears of the old mountaineer, now picked up the distant tumult.

"What is it?" Private Huffenberger whispered. "Sarge," he appealed to the veteran soldier, "what is it?"

Shorty spoke for Rick. "Ponies crossin' the river below camp." He laughed. "The boys ridin' in to make the guard think it's an Injun attack." He turned and gestured toward the bunk nearest the window. "About now, me and Sam should be up there, lettin' the rawhide down to Tom for the end of his trace chain."

Sam said stoutly, still gripping his stool. "We can still make it, Shorty. We're partners."

"You're also my brother," Rick cut in. "Don't forget that."

"A man," Sam said, "has to pick his own trail where it forks. This old dog here," he nodded toward Shorty, "has stood up for me many times against the world. He's covered me up plenty when I played the fool. Maybe I'm playin' the fool now, Rick. But he has the call on me."

The sound in the dusk was increasing. The crackling of brush could be heard as though horses were being forced through the willows along the river.

"We are not goin' out, Sam," Shorty said softly. "I meant what I said. We have split the blankets for keeps. I'm bad medicine for you, Sam, for here on out. What you need now is the Missoury cornfed to keep you on the straight and narrow—" He stopped talking. His eyes popped and his mouth gaped.

For the sound of a single shot cut the outside silence. Then a distant shout from the direction of the stables. "Post Number Four! Turn out the guard! *Injuns!*"

As though the alarm had unleashed all the hounds of hell, a wolf-like yelping choked off the sound of the shot and the sentry's yell.

"A good job for mule skinners," observed Spike Dillon.

"Gawd sakes!" cried Shorty. "That's the real thing. That's Sioux jumpin' us!"

Sam whirled and began to hammer on the door with the stool until it became a splintered wreck.

He groaned. "So much for the army," he said to Shorty. "Heavin' us in the mill. Nothing to fight with. To heck with your tall talk about peace and such. If I live to get out of here—"

Outside, the pounding of hoofs sounded loudly as horsemen swept through the lower edge of the camp. The war whoop rolled from painted throats. There was a scattering ragged volley of rifle fire like corn popping in a skillet. Then could be heard the bawling of the sentry at the post of the guard. "Turn out the guard! Number One! Turn out the guard! *Enemy in sight!*"

His hoarse shout was silenced by the brazen blaring of an army bugle. The musician of the guard had been booted out and set to blowing his instrument by some belted corporal. Sam recognised the thrilling notes of the call to arms. Along the line of tents, almost four companies of tough doughboys were turning out now, buckling up their cartridge belts, waiting, even in the midst of clamouring death, for the word of calm command.

"They got that sentry on Number Four," said Shorty. "But he got in his alarm first."

"How did you figure it as Sioux?" asked Sam.

"They're away down by the stables. We didn't figure to come that way. They'll set these soldiers afoot before the night's over."

Rick, assisted by Spike and Huffenberger, was pushing a set of bunks toward the door. He barked to the partners, "Come on and help."

"Give me a leg off that stool," said Shorty. "Maybe I can bust in a Sioux skull before they reach for my hair."

CHAPTER XXII

The men in the guard-house knew they had reached the end of their rope. They had barricaded the door with the bunks, but they understood this flimsy defence would yield quickly against the determined attack of maddened Sioux horsemen. They had prised boards off the bunk, and held them now, with the nails still sticking from the planking. Sam and Shorty had divided the stool between them.

"Go on and sing," Shorty said to Sam. "By cracklin', you always sung when we was in a tight. Go on and sing your buff'ler song, Sam."

Sam drew a deep breath. And then he began to sing softly, because there was no use trying to pitch his voice above the roaring of the fight outside, the spitting rattle of rifles, the ringing whoops of the Sioux, the beat of hoofs as the war ponies circled nearer to the guard-house.

> "Oh take me back to the buff'ler days,
> When Injuns whooped in the prairie haze,
> The West was wild and men died hard,
> But a man never quit on a good old pard!"

"Thanks, kid," drawled Shorty. "Thanks." And he raised the hem of his leather shirt and blew his nose and wiped out his eyes. "Thanks! By cracklin', a song to beat a war whoop!"

The door burst open. The noise of the fight poured in upon their ears like a flood torrent. Outside, the dusk was bright with fire. The rattle of rifles, the hoarse shouts of command, reached their ears. The bugle quit its braying, for now every man must fight.

Captain Budhouse stood framed in the doorway. He gripped a pistol. He was in his shirt. The Sioux had given the command no chance to turn out in fighting gear. They had cunningly staged their attack just before dusk when the soldiers were resting at ease, waiting for the supper mess call.

Dusk also suited the Sioux. It was not dark. The spirits would not be abroad to bring misfortune upon the Sioux.

"Sergeant!" roared the captain. "Sergeant! Clear the door! Take those men with you! Arm yourself at the post of the guard!"

"Yes, sir," said Rick.

"Make for the stables! Those hellions have fired the haystacks! They're trying to run off the mules and horses!"

Budhouse disappeared into the noise and smoke. He commanded four companies. He must hastily throw out a ring of steel around his camp, spur the faint-hearted, cheer on the brave. Many in that command had never heard the war whoop of a hostile Sioux or the deadly whir of a war arrow past his ear. Many there, like Private Huffenberger, had never been shot at. Tonight they would become veteran soldiers of the infantry. Tonight, in the fury of fire and the shock of gunfire, they would know what it took to be a doughboy.

Not a man objected when Rick assumed command. They thrust aside the bunks, went out the door on the run. The guard tent stood adjacent, between guard-house and the headquarters shack. The men of the guard, not on sentry duty, had been turned out and hurried down to posts along the river where brave men had died to sound the alarm.

A corporal was passing out Springfield rifles and cartridge belts from which cased bayonets dangled. Of all men, the corporal was Bootle. His hands were shaking and the sweat stood out on his fat face by the light of the smoky guard tent lantern. He choked out an objection when Rick and his grimy followers appeared, averring they were escaped prisoners.

But Rick took him by the throat and flung him aside. He began jerking the long single-shot rifles from the rack, pitching them to eager hands.

"I feel better," sighed Private Huffenberger. His hands were shaking also, and in the lantern light, his fresh-coloured

face now resembled a green cheese. But he buckled up his
belt, clicked his brogan heels together, and stood waiting for
orders.

"Fix your bayonets," rasped Rick. "Cold steel takes the
heart out of most Injuns!"

Shorty, untrained in army weapons, fumbled with the long
blade, cursing in a petulant way that he could do a better job
with a skinning knife.

The line of tents stood on high ground above the river. The
rear of the camp was dominated by a low ridge of sagebrush-
covered hills. Three hundred yards from the right flank of
the cantonment, the corrals and picket lines of the stables
had been established. They were on lower ground, and nearer
the river in order that stock could be watered more con-
veniently. Between the corrals and the tents ran the long road
that men called the Oregon Trail.

Sam helped Shorty fix his bayonet. The tip of the deadly
spike reached above the waspy little trapper's shaggy head.
Shorty had looped the cartridge belt over his shoulder,
bandolier fashion.

To the west, and down below the guard tent, near the
river brush, red flames flared up in the dusk. Black smoke
rolled eastward in the teeth of a brisk wind from the mountains, hampering the soldiers who were fighting on the left
flank of the camp. The Sioux had dismounted men, and sent
these crafty warriors crawling up through the brush to set
fire to the haystacks before they flung their mounted attack
across the river. They had known the fire and the smoke
would confuse and blind the pony soldiers and the
walkaheaps.

"That was one time," Shorty drawled, "when the army
and me agreed. When old Bughouse busted us out and told us
to git guns."

The army, Sam thought, had thrown him in the jail. But
in the pinch, it had also given him a chance to fight for his
life like a man. He had to grin. After this was over, if he still
lived, the army would send another detail to arrest him and

throw him back in the mill. He could cover himself with glory in the fight tonight, but that wouldn't save him from the mill. The army never changed. Men changed—but never the army.

"Dumb," Sam said softly, "but dogged."

He slanted his gaze about, using the eyes of an expert in Indian fighting. He believed this attack would be beaten off. the powwow had decided, at Paint Rock, to alarm the cantonment garrison and pin it down, thus giving Canada Pete leeway for the delivery of his magazine rifles and ammunition to the Kicking Horse.

This was the day of the second sleep. Any time on the morrow, Canada Pete would make the meet with the Kicking Horse at the Wolf Creek crossing.

The Sioux had drawn back immediately along Sam's front. Doughboys, deploying, had begun a slow advance toward the brush along the river. Now and then, a Springfield boomed. There was also some sort of a fight going on at the far end of the line of tents, but Sam didn't concern himself about that. Plenty of soldiers down there to save their hair and their packs.

But west, and around the blazing haystacks, a continual clamour of battle arose from the stable guard. A few men fighting to hold off warriors anxious to reach the ponies and mules.

"If the war whoops had magazine rifles," Sam said to Shorty, "by this time they'd have all the hair of those guards down there."

Rick flung himself from the guard tent. He was pushing Bootle ahead. Bootle's jaw wagged as he stuttered that he was on duty, charged with issuing guns.

"Everything's passed out now," Rick said grimly. "You and me was together once on another raid. You didn't like the way I performed then. I want to give you a show now to prove how brave you are. Men are needed at the stables. Come along with us!"

The fire flared higher in the burning stacks. The light

illuminated the set faces of Rick's forlorn command. It out-
lined the scurrying forms of horsemen, darting from brush
along the river, circling along the rim of the red light cast
from the stable area.

"Take out in single file," Rick barked, his harsh voice
ringing above the continual clamour of shrill war whoops, the
bark of guns, the pounding of pony hoofs. "I'll take the lead
with Sam and Shorty. Don't open fire until I pass the word.
Light's bad. Target's out of good range."

He started off at a dogtrot, Sam and Shorty close at his
heels, the soldiers next in line.

Rick, with an old soldier's skill, took advantage of shadows
and covering brush as he quartered down the gentle slope
toward the stables. Intent on reaching the mules and ponies,
the Sioux didn't sight the hard-running detail until Rick
reached the broad circle of firelight.

Sioux horsemen, sighting the line of men, made a rush.
They drove in to cut between Rick's detail and the stables.
War arrows whizzed past. One red rider hanging low from the
back of his pony let go with an old brass-bound trade musket.

"Yagh!" the warriors whooped. "Yagh!"

Rick turned his head, barked sharply, "Halt! Face to your
left! Commence firing!"

Sam, obeying, dropped to one knee, pitching the Springfield
stock to his shoulder. He missed the Henry, but it was good
to feel the shock of the army gun against his shoulder as he
aimed, then pulled the trigger.

Shorty knelt at his side. He hadn't fired. In the approved
style of old Indian fighters, he waited for his partner to let go,
then fired while the friend reloaded. That way, Indians could
not draw bullets, then rush in and cut down opponents
between volleys.

In the uncertain light, and firing on mounted men, Sam
wasn't sure that he had hit a living target. But he grinned
and calmly thrust a finger-long shell into his rifle chamber.
Shorty was taking his time getting the feel of the balance and
hang of an unfamiliar weapon.

"The danged bay'nit," he said, from the corner of his mouth, "sorta pulls the front sight down. Out'n kilter. Man wants to allow for that."

Private Huffenberger, not yet a veteran, put his first bullet into the earth ten feet from where he was crouching. Rick Sling, ranging up and down his line, head and shoulders up, bent and patted the rookie on the shoulder as the sweating lad fumbled in reloading. "Take it easy, son," he admonished. "We got all night to whip 'em. Get your sights in line. Then hold and squeeze!"

"Ye-yes sir," stammered Huffenberger.

Spike Dillon, siding the recruit, fired slowly and calmly. A war arrow hit the earth directly in front of him and hung there, shaft quivering. Spike, shifting his aim, knocked the bowman off his pony.

Bootle leaped up, quavering. "I'm headin' for the stables! They'll ride over us here!"

Rick tried to slap Bootle into line. "Keep your head down," he ordered.

Bootle broke away. He bolted away from the line, seeking to gain the shelter of the stable. He stopped as though he had bumped into a rock. A war arrow caught him in the throat. He plunged forward with a clatter of belt and arms. Huffenberger, aiming, dropped his rifle point, turned his head aside, lost his supper.

Spike Dillon, reaching out, slapped him on the back. "That's right, lad," he said heartily. "Lighten yourself for the fight!"

"Gah!" panted Huffenberger. But he raised the Springfield with shaking hands and fired.

"Good!" yelled Dillon, telling a blessed white lie. "You knocked that big Sioux buck gallivantin'."

"Sure enough?" breathed Huffenberger.

"Sure as I'm a church member," said Spike.

Sam and Shorty saw Bootle die with the arrow in his throat. They exchanged not a word. They centred their gunfire on the riders who were striving to cut them off from the stable.

Sam bored a pony. Shorty dropped a warrior. That took off the flank pressure.

"Now!" Rick yelled. "Make for the stable!"

They reached the lines and flopped down, panting like hard-run dogs, on the flank of a line of sweating, cursing soldiers and civilians.

"Pete sakes!" cried old Shorty. "Red Dog and Jake! What you mule skinners doin' here?"

"Your pard, Tom, organised us to help you bust out'n the guard-house. But as we got set the danged Sioux took the play away from us."

"Where's Tom?"

"Ain't seen him. Us boys busted down here to help out."

The Sioux had already reached some of the outside picket lines and stampeded the horses. But the frightened braying mules, hating Indian smell, had bunched up around the old grey bell mare. Wisps of burning hay, carried from the blazing stacks, now and then lit on a mule's nervous back, driving the beast to the point of madness from pain.

CHAPTER XXIII

The bulk of the mule herd was saved by a small force of experts including Jake and Red Dog. Sam went along with them. They led the bell mare into the pole corral. The mules, a good thirty head, trailed after her. At the gate of the corral, Sam encountered Lieutenant Prime. Fire and smoke and sweat had taken all the polish off his uniform. A slug from an Indian musket had broken his right arm between elbow and wrist. Prime was half mad with pain and vexation at the loss of his ponies. But he had fashioned a sling for his arm from his neck scarf and was wobbling around, keeping his men in line.

"Whole detail's here," he told Sam. "Ordered in from the trading post for remounts."

"Who's guardin' the wagon train?"

"Plenty of teamsters there."

"But most of those mule skinners are here tonight."

Given this information, Prime became alarmed. "What'll become of Miss Payne?" he wanted to know. "What'll become of her?"

"I don't think the Sioux'll hit the post. That's Pete's property. This is just a small force of Injuns sent in to bother the army so it won't keep an eye on Pete."

"We'll mount up on mules," said Prime. He shouted to the grimy stable sergeant to select some mules that had been broken to ride and to saddle them up.

But Sam shook his head. The Indian attack was at its height. A group of riders could not break through.

"We can try it!" the lieutenant raged, and shouted for the saddling detail to hurry the work.

A knot of Sioux riders, angered that the mules had escaped them, rode down boldly. War arrows whizzed, clattering against the rails of the corral. Sam dropped to his knees, thrusting out an arm and attempting to pull down the lieutenant. Prime dropped but not through Sam's aid. An arrow snapped into his left shoulder. He was totally disabled. His six-shooter dropped from his hand as he fell, and Sam scooped it up.

Sam called to a soldier dodging past him, rifle cocked for a fast shot. "Take care of your loot. He's bad hurt. Put him in the shade!"

Sam turned and crawled back to his place in the line. As he dropped down between Shorty and Red Dog, he heard his friends cursing. A bugle was blaring from brush down by the river.

"Some danged deserter," growled Red Dog. "I wisht I could see him to shoot."

"No deserter," said Sam. "If you saw him, he'd be wearin' a blue coat. That's Pete."

"Pete?" cried Red Dog "But he was in on the deal to help you get out. Him and Chicago Jack. Both of 'em orter be here. Jack told us, after we got you and Shorty out, you'd show us a secret trail to Montany. If this Injun deal hadn't busted out, we'd be hookin' up now to start north.''

So that was why Jack had wished to draw Sam into some sort of a deal. To act as a guide on another attempt to crack the army deadline.

The steady fire from the front of the corral turned back the Indian attack. The Sioux withdrew sullenly to the brush, uttering derisive yells as they rode off. But they would come again.

There ensued a space which didn't seem long to Sam. There were wounded men to care for, dead men to be dragged back and covered up with saddle blankets.

Near midnight, the dirty, red-eyed stable sergeant broke out some rations of fat bacon and hard tack which his grimy followers wolfed down. The main attack had either been broken or the Sioux horsemen had withdrawn with the herd of ponies they had stolen. A few bold warriors still lingered in the river thickets, mostly armed with trade muskets.

Sam and Shorty had decided that, with the garrison again in command of the situation, they would attempt to break through the lines. They would not trust to mules. They'd take the trail afoot. Only a mile to go to reach the trading post. Sam retained Prime's pistol. He had not wasted cartridges from it. He had depended upon the army rifle. Shorty borrowed a hand gun from Red Dog, and a few rounds of extra ammunition.

They were talking over their plan for the break when a dim figure came weaving up from the river, half seen in the dancing light of the fire from the stacks which had now subsided to red beds of glowing embers.

"An Injun!" Red Dog said bitterly, and fired.

The Indian came on. He began to yell. "Shoshone! Shoshone!"

Shorty struck down the barrel of the mule skinner's gun. "That's Tom!" he yelled. "He's hurt! Hold your fire!"

Shorty leaped like a rabbit from the line. He began to run

toward his faltering partner. Sam was close at his heels. But Tom was nearer the far western end of the deployed line than to their position.

They saw, as they ran, the ungainly figure of a soldier speeding toward the staggering Shoshone.

"Rick!" panted Sam. "Old Rick!"

Rick, reaching Tom, put his arm around the Indian, trying to help him in a run for the firing line. A gun boomed from the river. Rick took his arm from Tom. He sagged at the knees and went down.

Sam and Shorty brought in the wounded men.

Rick had been shot through the body. Tom Bear Mouth carried a broken off war arrow in his right shoulder. Not a serious wound, but hard, long trailing had weakened the Shoshone, and the wound had sapped his strength. The farrier sergeant, who dealt with diseases and hurts of horses and mules, tied up the hole in Rick and observed gruffly to Sam that he thought the old sergeant would make a go of it. "He's tough," he said. "Put him over here where the heat won't reach him."

They laid out Rick and Tom in cool shadows. Prime was there, gritting his teeth against pain, striving to cheer up his disabled men. Sam bent over his brother while Shorty listened to Tom.

"Can you talk, Rick?" he asked.

"Sure, boy! Always good at talkin'." Rick smiled faintly. "As you've often said. What's on your mind?"

"Farrier sergeant says you'll make the grade, Rick. That was a danged brave thing you did. Savin' the life of an Injun."

"Injun," breathed Rick. "Well, I'll be danged. I heard him yell for help and I went for him." He grinned. "It might have been Huffenberger, you know."

"Rick, they'll take care of you now. I've got to go. With Shorty."

"Where, boy?"

"Canada Pete was here with the Sioux earlier. But I don't

think he's around now. This is comin' on to the third sleep when he makes the gun deal with the Sioux. They've coaxed away all the civilians from the train. There's white women out there."

"And a Missoury cornfed," whispered Rick. He raised his right hand weakly. "Well, boy, this time I won't try to stop you from goin' over the hill."

It required hours of careful scouting to slip through the night to their goal. They yearned to stand on their legs and run. But Sioux might be in camp any place along this ridge they were following. They held grimly to shadows and cover, depending on their rangecraft.

Dawn was breaking when they crawled down from the crest of the brushy hill that loomed to the rear of Pete's post. Their eager eyes checked on the buildings and the vehicles of the train. The place had not been attacked.

Sam gave silent thanks.

When they reached the trading post, Little Bird, Pete's wife, met them. They entered the cabin and found the Night Star bedded down on the dirt floor. Sunset Liz and her girls were ministering to the Indian woman, whose eyes were bright with fever.

"Poor thing," said Sunset Liz. "But she'll live. She come down here to knife Canada Pete. But Pete and that double-dealin' Chicago Jack had pulled out."

"Pulled out?" cried Sam. "When?"

"First crack of day. Half-hour ago. They took that Missoury gal with 'em. Pete took her away from her guardeen at gun point. Chicago Jack thinks Pete knows a secret trail to Montany. Since they had to travel fast and light, they only took my wagon." Liz curled a bitter lip. "My barrel of pain killer in it."

Shorty, who had been roving around outside, came in. He had discovered blocks of ice and brush used for insulation round the ice-house entrance.

"That's where Pete has his guns cached," said Sam. "Army searched and got down to the ice, likely. Guns and ca'tridges hid under the ice. Safe even if the ice-house caught fire."

Little Bird touched Sam on the arm. She drew him aside. "Pete like too many women," she said. "I show you trail. Old Sioux trail. He go to meet my brother."

"Who's your brother, Little Bird?"

"He wild boy. He called Kicking Horse."

"We'll take a couple of these mules, Little Bird. Pete won't be expectin' anybody to chase him so early."

Shorty wished to ride, but Sam declared it was Shorty's duty to ride herd on the women in the trading post. Undoubtedly a relief party from the cantonment would soon arrive. But Pete must be halted, the Missouri girl rescued, and, at all costs, the Kicking Horse prevented from receiving the renegade guns and shells.

Sam and Little Bird rode away from the post.

CHAPTER XXIV

Through the craft of Little Bird, the pursuers overtook Pete and Chicago Jack in a rocky little draw where sagebrush grew high on the surrounding hills. Little Bird was in the lead. Wrapped in a blanket she appeared to the white men like an Indian messenger appearing with word of the place where the guns and cartridges would be turned over to the Kicking Horse.

Chicago Jack was riding his pony alongside the lumbering wagon. Canada Pete was on the high seat, driving the four head of labouring mules. Little Bird rode in from the flank, blanket fluttering in the wind. Her face was calm, inscrutable. Her appearance startled Pete. He reined down his teams and set his brake.

"Go on back," he ordered harshly. "You ain't wanted out here!"

Little Bird made no reply. She checked her mule and

waited while Sam Sling, riding past, with drawn hand gun, called to Chicago Jack, "You wanted me in on this deal, Jack. Remember when we talked about it up the country?"

Jack cursed and reined his horse around to face Sam. He reached for his holstered gun, but Sam's Colt was lined upon him.

"I didn't figure, Jack, that the deal we talked over meant selling guns and shells to Sioux Injuns. Or runnin' off with white women."

Jack's face was contorted with rage. He was watching Sam, waiting for a break.

"I don't know nothing about renegade guns," he said. "The wagon's loaded with flour and bales of beaver pelts. And a big barrel of pain killer. We aim to get to Montany, Sam."

"How about the Payne girl?"

Jack grinned wolfishly. "Maybe she yearned to come with us, Sam. She's back there restin' soft on them beaver pelts."

"I know where Pete got those pelts," said Sam. "The pelts and the girl are coverin' up the rifles and shells he figures to deliver soon to the Kicking Horse. And most likely, Jack, when he turns that trick, you'll lose your hair."

Jack turned his head and called up to Pete, who sat grinning slyly on the wagon seat. "You didn't say nothing about guns, Pete. Are you double-crossin' me?"

"So long, Jack," drawled Pete, and he whipped up a hand gun and shot Jack between the eyes. Jack reeled, fell from his pony. His left toe caught in the stirrup. The horse, alarmed by the bark of Pete's gun, stampeded, dragging the dead body after it.

Pete turned on Sam, swinging up the smoking gun.

"Your war medicine ain't strong enough, Sam," he started to say.

Something whirred through the air. A war arrow drove through the breast of Pete. His gun exploded, but his bullet was wild. His body twisted to the side, and dropped from the high seat to the earth.

Little Bird rode up, calm of face. She carried a bow. She stared down at Pete, who lay on his back with the painted arrow shaft protruding from his body.

"He no good," Little Bird said. "Too many women." She touched her breast. "Me—I'm his wife!"

A girl screamed in the wagon. Sam found Jane Payne in the wagon box, tied up, laid out on bales of beaver pelts. Pelts that had once been on stretchers in the Big Horns. Beneath the girl and the pelts, Sam found several wooden cases that contained magazine rifles and boxes of ammunition.

He freed Jane. She was wide-eyed, and almost speechless with fear. He helped her from the wagon. She shuddered and turned her eyes away from the form of Canada Pete. The Indian woman led her away from the wagon consoling her.

Sam's first thought was to turn the wagon and head back for the post. Not a far distance. The mule teams had not stirred at the roll of gunfire. For Pete had set his brake before he killed his man.

Then Sam heard the cry of Jane Payne. "Sam—Indians are coming!"

Peering out the front of the wagon, from under the canvas top stretched over hickory hoops, he saw horsemen in the distance, slipping down through the brush. The Kicking Horse was coming for his guns.

He shouted to Jane to mount up on his mule, ride with Little Bird for the post. He didn't hear her answer. There was no time for talk if he was to prevent the Indians from seizing the guns and shells.

An axe was fastened to the back of the wagon seat. There was a quick method of touching off a fire. Sam took the axe and beat open the head of the big wooden barrel of painkiller. He tilted the barrel and let its contents gush over the stack of pelts, and the cased guns and cartridges beneath. When the barrel was empty, he recalled that Liz had told him that Jack had desired to get to Montana because of the barrel's contents. But surely one lone barrel of trade whisky wouldn't induce a frontiersman to risk his scalp.

So Sam wasn't surprised when he drew two leather bags of gold coins from the barrel of pain killer. That meant Pete and Jack had been pards in the raid on the paymaster. Sam pitched the bags of coins from the wagon. If the army ever came up, they'd find some evidence that would clear old Rick of any involvement in the raid.

Then Sam took out a block of sulphur matches, struck one, and when it had taken on a good red glow, dropped it into the whisky-soaked pile of pelts. Then he stepped down from the wagon, unhitched the mules, drew his hand gun, and prepared to meet the Sioux.

They were coming on slowly, he saw. They were still a quarter-mile distant when the fire in the wagon flared up. They made a nervous circle when the flames reached the boxes of cartridges and the shells began exploding.

Then they rode up, not on the run, but slowly. Sam met them. And Jane Payne stood at his side, for she hadn't run away. Little Bird was there also, wrapped in her blanket, standing unconcerned over the sprawled body of Canada Pete.

Sam saw the Kicking Horse. The war chief was burning with rage as he came riding on, leading a dozen of his warriors. And with the party were old Sioux braves in blankets and paint and feathers.

While he watched the approaching Indians Sam said softly to Jane Payne, "There's five live loads in this gun, Jane. Prime handed it to me."

"Good for the lieutenant." She was brave. "Save the last two loads, Sam."

"The first then for the Kicking Horse. That one over there with the pony painted on his brisket."

"I wish you could sing to me, Sam. Your buffalo song."

"I can't think of a good verse right now, Jane. But you know what I'm thinkin'. Of all the little gals from old Missoury—"

"Cornfeds," she whispered.

He broke it off. The Sioux had halted. An old man came

forward on a pacing pony. The old man carried an eagle plume fan, and the tail of his eagle feather war bonnet reached to the top of the sagebrush. The aged chief was poising a long lance. Slowly Sam raised the pistol and lined on the Kicking Horse.

Then Little Bird stepped aside, revealing the body of Canada Pete, and the painted arrow that protruded from his body. She talked to the old chief with hand signs, and in the Sioux lingo. When she had ended, the old chief looked at Sam and the Missouri girl. Then he rode over and spat on the body of Pete.

"He no good," the chief said calmly.

The Kicking Horse drove his pony forward. Then he saw Pete's body and the arrow in it. He checked his mount. Rage gripped him. But he turned aside when the old chief touched his pony on the withers with the eagle plume fan.

Without another word, the Sioux turned their horses and rode slowly off into the hills.

"And there," Sam rasped, breathing sharply as though he had run a mile, "goes your Sioux war."

"What happened?" Jane whispered. She was unsteady on her legs now that danger had passed, and Sam steadied her with his arms on her shoulders.

"That old chief," he said, "was the father of the Kickin' Horse and Little Bird. He never was strong for any war. He had argued against it with other old men, but Pete's guns was the ace in the hole of the Kickin' Horse and the younger bucks. But Pete got too prosperous when he tried to run out on a high-born Sioux woman like Little Bird. She sure told her father plenty about him. And that was enough to show them that Pete had been bad medicine for the Sioux from the start."

The relief column, under old Captain Budhouse, rounded up the rags and tags of the fight with the Sioux by late afternoon. Budhouse met Sam and Jane Payne and the recent widow of Canada Pete when they finally came into the post.

He rode back with Sam to the scene of the burning of the wagon. The bags of gold were there, evidence clearing up the raid on the pay coach.

Private Huffenberger and Spike Dillon were in the detail, glad at last they'd get paid off. Twisted metal parts of rifles were found in the charred ruins of the wagon, effectively pinning down Canada Pete as a renegade. And the marks on the arrow driven into his evil heart matched those on the broken bits of shaft which Rick had carried in his pocket.

Returned to the post, Captain Budhouse met a frightened girl.

"I suppose," she said to him, "you'll arrest Sam now for stealing your old horse."

Budhouse turned a grim eye on Sam, and then he smiled. "I regret to tell you, Miss Payne," he said, "that Corporal Dillon will not sign an affidavit. He states, under oath, that he could not identify the man who stole his horse. So—the army is forced to give a clearance to Sam Sling. And ma'am, hereafter, keep him to the straight and narrow and out of the guard-house. His brother's alive and will make the grade. He'd wish me to tell you that."

Shorty and Tom Bear Mouth rode slowly past the trading post, pointing their ponies toward the west and the Continental Divide. The Night Star was with them, hiding her face in her blanket but riding straight in the saddle. The bad medicine man who had betrayed her and her husband was gone. And this old Shorty, he would be kind to the grieving Night Star.

Little Bird, now sole proprietor of the post, was inside the cabin dealing out goods to mule skinners and soldiers. The soldiers now had gold to spend.

"Sing us a farewell song, Sam," Shorty said.

Sam reached for the tough hand of his old partner.

"I can't sing," he said. "For once in my life, I can't sing, Shorty. But long life and good camps, old friend."

Before he rode on, Shorty took something off his saddle. He handed it down to Sam. It was a blue army blouse.

"We found it inside Pete's cabin," he said. "You can give it back to the good soldier who lost it. Your brother Rick."

"What about the old bugle?"

"It never showed up. Maybe Pete lost it in the river fight. But wherever it is, you can bet the Kicking Horse no longer figures it is good medicine."

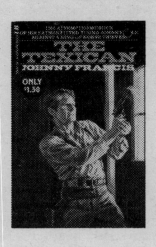

THE TEXICAN
By Johnny Francis

PRICE: $1.50 LB750
CATEGORY: Western

Johnny Dale lived a quiet hardworking life on a Texas ranch until double-barreled trouble exploded in his face. A band of horse thieves wanted Johnny's father dead. Young Johnny found himself with only one chance to clear his name and to bring his father's enemies to justice!

RIO GRANDE RIPTIDE
By Roe Richmond

PRICE: $1.75 LB734
CATEGORY: Western (original)

Texas Ranger Lash Lashtrow is sent to the Mexican border to investigate a series of brutal murders of Mexican women. He is joined by a young Mexican boy, "Chico" Canitas—the son of one of the murdered women—and his old compadre, Rusty Bouchard. Lashtrow soon narrows his suspects to two men, the Iselin brothers, hoping they will lead him to the mind behind the crimes. They do—and Lashtrow finds himself up against the most deadly enemy he has ever encountered!

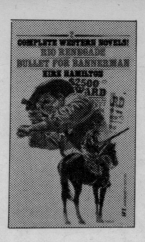

RIO RENEGADE and BULLET FOR BANNERMAN
By Kirk Hamilton

PRICE: $2.25 LB726
CATEGORY: Western

In RIO RENEGADE, Yancey Bannerman, the
Enforcer, and Johnny Cato join forces in pursuit
of a renegade called the Bearcat. Cato captures
the outlaw, but loses him—and nearly loses his
own life. It's up to Bannerman to catch up with
the Bearcat and bring him in—dead or alive! In
BULLET FOR BANNERMAN, ranchowner Tris-
tram Griffin is Bannerman's most deadly enemy—
and with good reason. The Enforcer had maimed
Griffin and eliminated his henchmen, leaving the
bitter bad man with no choice but to strike back at
the law and the lawmen who had caused him
grief!